WESLEY ELLIS

LONE STAR

ON THE
TREACHERY TRAIL

J.

A JOVE BOOK

LONE STAR ON THE TREACHERY TRAIL

A Jove Book / published by arrangement with
the author

PRINTING HISTORY
Jove edition / September 1982

ISBN: 0-515-06226-X

PRINTED IN THE UNITED STATES OF AMERICA

LONE STAR

ON THE TREACHERY TRAIL

Chapter 1

The sudden spring storm broke with a thunderclap across southeastern Wyoming. Descending out of Canada and through Montana like a last savage howl of winter, the gale swept in on ugly, bloated clouds and torrential rains, darkening the sky until only a flashing lacework of lightning revealed the looming peaks of the Laramie Range and its wind-whipped foothills, thick with saltbush, cottonwood, and mountain mahogany.

The North Laramie River was a twisting, whorling tide, swelling from the abrupt and unexpected runoff. Paralleling and occasionally crossing the river was a rutted, muddy trail that connected Uva and Garrett and the few smaller cow towns in between, and slowly churning westward along it was a Special Pontiac closed wagon, pulled by two Jenny Lind—bridled Morgans. Obliquely slashing rain beat against the wagon's seasoned wood sides and heavy duck roof, and

1

savagely gusting wind tore at its rubberized curtains that were rolled down and fastened front and rear. And despite its wide stance—seven feet long by three feet wide, with a five-foot track—and its easy-rolling, forty-two-inch high Sarven's Patent wheels, its team constantly had to shift and thrust to keep the wagon on course through the gumbo.

The body of the wagon was painted a ruby-wine color with vermillion striping, making it resemble the sort of rig a snake-oil drummer might use to ply his elixirs. The two who were riding on the buffed leather-upholstered front seat, however, were anything but traveling medicine men.

Concentrating with the reins in both hands was a lean man in his early thirties, his blue-gray suit swathed in an oilskin slicker, his Stetson tugged low against the weather. Shadowed by the hatbrim, his features bore that handsome quality which appeals to women who like their men tempered by experience and bronzed by sun. There was a seriousness about him, too, the glint of chilled steel in his almond eyes and a terseness to his thin lips—all of which would have indicated to a close and knowledgeable observer that one of this man's parents had been Oriental; and that the mating of East and West had produced a proud, rugged, quiet yet determined individual who blended the best of both worlds. He fit well the name he'd adopted when he'd arrived in America: *Ki,* the Japanese word for the vital energy that suffuses all living things, and the mastery of which is the true warrior's life-work.

His passenger was a tall, lissome woman in her twenties; her father had hired Ki to be her companion and guardian some years before. Like Ki, Jessica Starbuck was wearing a rain slicker, its yellowish color almost matching her long coppery-blonde hair, which she'd tucked up under the crown of her brown Stetson. And although the slicker was buttoned at the neck and completely covered her green tweed jacket and skirt, it did little to conceal her firm, jutting breasts and sensuously rounded thighs and buttocks. Her mother, Sarah, had been a redheaded beauty who'd passed to her daughter a long-limbed, lushly molded figure covered in flesh as

2

creamy and flawless as ivory, and a cameo face with a pert nose and more than a hint of feline audacity to her wide-set green eyes. Yet Jessie's father, Alex Starbuck, had given a steadfastness to her dimpled chin and a shrewd if sometimes humorous twist to her lips. Even though both parents were dead—murdered and subsequently avenged—in a very real sense they lived on, embodied in the spirit and actions of their only offspring.

And whatever might be claimed about Jessie Starbuck's spirit and actions, hawking patent snake oil out of a wagon couldn't be included. She'd had the wagon custom-built and fancied up to her specifications; she had to take the blame or credit if its purpose was mistaken. But other than a few personal belongings, which barely filled the small leather trunk wedged behind the seat, there was nothing in the wagon that she felt was hers—except that generally, everything bought in the name of Starbuck was hers.

Nonetheless, Jessie had wanted the wagon along, and had freighted it with them when she and Ki had taken the Union Pacific to Cheyenne four days ago. After spending the first night in the bustling territorial capital, they had hired the harness team and begun a grueling upcountry trek, stopping the second night at Underwood and the third night at Wheatland, before reaching Uva and turning west. They'd traveled well over a hundred miles, and estimated they still had another ten or so to go before arriving at their destination, the small valley cow town of Eucher Butte.

It would be there, at Eucher Butte, that the wagon would come in handy, if it didn't prove to be downright lifesaving. Because, for all practical purposes, the wagon belonged to Ki, and it was where, in racks and cabinets, he stored some of his considerable collection of lethal weapons.

Sired in Japan by an American "barbarian" who'd taken for his wife a Japanese woman of nobility, Ki had been orphaned at an early age. A half-breed outcast, shamed yet stubborn, he had apprenticed himself to one of the last samurai, Hirata, who for a decade drilled Ki in unarmed combat, and trained him in the use of *kyujutsu, kenjutsu,*

3

bojutsu, jojutsu, and *shuriken-jutsu*—the martial arts of bow and arrow, sword, staff, stick, and throwing knife—as well as in even more exotic techniques and devices.

Such were the weapons, in their numerous variations, that Ki stowed in the otherwise innocuous-appearing wagon. Others he kept on his person, like the *shuriken,* steel disks in the shape of razor-sharp stars, attached in spring-loaded releases to his wrists. Still others, such as his *katana,* the sword left to him by Hirata, Ki preferred to leave behind in the safety of the huge Starbuck ranch in Texas.

Packed with death as the wagon was, its purpose was not to start wars, but to end them as swiftly and victoriously as possible. Neither Ki nor Jessica relished violence. Yet, as Hirata had taught Ki, and Ki in turn had taught Jessica: "To fight with another is wrong, but to lose a fight with another over principles you deem honorable is worse." They had no intention of losing any fight forced upon them.

Ki snapped the traces smartly, goading the Morgans into lunging against their hames and collars. The wagon swayed, lurching on its elliptical springs, its oil lamps shining blurred and dim through the sheets of driven rain. Forked shards of lightning did more to illuminate the trail ahead, and Ki was able to glimpse in their intermittent flashes where the ribbon of mud crested a ridge overlooking the river, and avoided a bouldered cliff by crossing over to the other side on a narrow plank bridge. The North Laramie, deep in its cutbanks, roared in an angry torrent, chunks of trees and uprooted bushes sweeping past, bucking and weaving, careening and jamming against the bridge supports before plummeting on down through the white-water channel.

Jessie, seeing the bridge shuddering from the impact of the water and debris, called over the fury of the storm: "You think it's safe enough to cross?"

Ki shrugged. "No way to tell, unless we stop and inspect it," he answered, as the team headed into the curve. "Do you want to?"

"Let's chance it. The bridge isn't very long, maybe fifty feet or so, and we're relatively light." She started to smile

4

and then laughed out loud. "Remember this morning, when I wondered if it might rain before we reached Eucher Butte?"

"I remember. You hoped it would."

"Well, don't hold it against me. I was in the mood for a little breezy sprinkle, not a downpour. Now I hope it'll just go away."

"It should. It's moving south pretty fast and—"

"Look out!"

But Ki was already aware of the danger, having spotted it a split second before Jessica's shouted warning. The wagon was slewing and skidding around the sharp turn leading to the bridge; the roadbed was poorly banked and wickedly slippery from rain. Ki rode the footbrake and snugged the reins, the treacherous, storm-masked angle requiring all his attention and dexterity.

And the two men emerging onto the trail in front of them undoubtedly knew it. Garbed in nondescript slickers and sodden hats, they raised repeating carbines to their shoulders and began firing a head-on fusillade at the onrushing wagon. In the same instant, two other men rose from the boulders flanking the curve, and started shooting from each side as fast as they could trigger and lever.

"Duck!" Ki yelled, kicking off the brake and lashing the reins, hunching as low as he could while salvoes of lead punctured the curtain behind them and riddled the wooden body with splintering holes. The ambushers had chosen well, he realized fleetingly; they'd planned on the rocks here to give them shelter while hemming in the trail, and had counted on his having his hands literally full just keeping the wagon from toppling over—too full to be able to fight back.

But the bridge ahead was clear. If a tree or some boulders had been thrown across the roadbed, the trap would have been perfect, forcing the wagon to halt or crash. Perhaps there hadn't been time, or there weren't any trees nearby and the rocks were too large to shift, or the gunmen hadn't wanted to risk a forewarning, and figured their ambush was good enough as it was—whatever their reason, they'd neglected to barricade the trail beyond their gantlet.

All this Ki deduced in the blink of an eye.

"We're going to try driving through them," he shouted, urging the team on faster. "Be ready to jump and run if we start to roll over. At the rate we're going, we're liable to, but it's our only hope." *And a pretty dismal one at that,* he thought, grimacing as he battled the wheel-twisting, hub-squealing, erratically tipping wagon. He glanced at Jessica, who was sitting upright on the seat. "For God's sake, Jessie, get down!"

"I *was* down," she replied with a mirthless smile, cocking her two-shot .38 derringer. She had been down crouching behind the curved metal dashboard even as Ki had been first yelling for her to duck—but only long enough to reach up underneath her slicker and skirt to where she wore the derringer gartered to her thigh. Her other pistol, a custom .38 double-action Colt on a .44 frame, was packed in her trunk, it being too bulky and uncomfortable to wear on a long trip. It had been a logical decision at the time she'd packed it, but now it made her curse with frustration.

The wagon continued bearing down on the gunmen in front, leaning to the point of falling, swaying and lurching, throwing off their aim. Bracing herself against the seat, trying to keep her precarious balance, Jessica held her fire, not about to waste her bullets on bobbing targets out of the meager range of her hideout gun.

The man flanking her side of the trail came sprinting diagonally toward them, apparently figuring to intercept the wagon before it could go any farther. He rushed forward, clawing for a handhold, so close that Jessica could see his stubbled, thick-lipped face, and his lidded eyes gleaming with certain victory over a defenseless woman.

She brought the derringer up, caught her right wrist with her left hand, and took a bead on his chest. Her finger squeezed the trigger. The sound of her shot was hardly more than the snap of a finger, lost in the raging storm around them. The man screamed hoarsely and fell back to lie in

6

the mud, inert and unfeeling as the rear wheel of the wagon jounced over him.

The bullet-spooked Morgans surged into their collars, dragging the wildly tottering wagon in frantic jerks. The two men in front and the man on Ki's side were still lined up and firing away. At such close range, both Ki and Jessica should have been riddled like sieves, but the swaying and lurching of the wagon made accurate firing impossible. The wagon was an inferno of flying lead, wood spraying in tiny slivers, the metal dashboard denting from ricocheting bullets. A slug burned along Ki's left arm, raising an ugly welt. But he kept on leashing the frightened team toward the bridge, and the two men in front suddenly realized he wasn't about to stop and let them shoot him, and if they stayed where they were, they'd likely get run over.

The men sprang aside, still firing up at the wagon. The one nearest to Ki dove for the on-side Morgan as it galloped past, in what was evidently a crazy maneuver to stop the team. He caught hold of the side strap and began running clumsily alongside in an effort to get a better grip and swing the horse off stride. The horse shied, sending the wagon into a sideways skid, and for a moment it seemed that the man would succeed. But he had misjudged the speed of the team and the nearness of the bridge. The Morgans lunged onto the planks, the horse with its clinging man grazing the bridge railing. His body was flattened, his single cry of shock and pain cut off as his chest was crushed. The horse dragged him another few feet, his fingers trapped in the strap, then smeared him once again against the railing. His body catapulted into the air, tumbling up over the railing and down into the river.

The wagon careened against the same railing, almost tearing off a wheel, then straightened and lurched, clattering, onto the bridge.

"We made it," Jessie said, smiling broadly.

Ki shook his head. "There's a man in back."

How Ki could sense such a thing over all the commotion

7

and howling storm completely baffled Jessica, but she didn't question it. From long experience she'd learned to trust Ki's uncommon abilities, and she took it on faith that one of the two remaining gunmen had managed to grab the tailgate and climb aboard, and was now lurking in the closed bed of the wagon. She turned on the seat, derringer ready.

And the man launched his attack through the tattered curtain, firing his sixgun directly at her. But already Jessica was pivoting farther to one side so she could see behind her; her action was so swift he had not reacted to it, so he fired at where she had been.

Simultaneously, Ki killed him. His eyes were focused straight ahead at the trembling plank bridgeway, but suddenly, before either Jessica or the man could trigger again, the reins were in his left hand, and his right was slashing back. It was a hand hardened by years of training, and now it sliced unerringly like the edge of an executioner's axe, chopping against the man's throat, crushing his larnyx and cracking his spine.

The man crouched there with his pistol in his hand, staring at Jessica in sheer disbelief, paralyzed in death. Without a sound he rolled sideways as his left leg buckled under him, and toppled back out of sight behind the curtain.

Shaken, Jessie asked, "Any more?"

"Yes," Ki answered, eyes still on the bridge. "But not with us."

"Only one, though."

"Here, perhaps. But these four were hired, Jessie, they weren't the brains. Likely the last man is already going for the horses they hid, and'll be riding to report their failure."

"Eucher Butte. He'll be heading there."

"Assuming he does, he'll be on this trail behind us, faster than us. Or if he's stupid, he might simply try to pursue us and cut us down before we reach Eucher Butte."

"Which do you think?"

"Stupid," Ki said flatly, recalling the lack of a barricade.

"Either way, if we do get to Eucher Butte alive, we'll be prime targets for plenty more treachery."

Ki gave Jessie a flinty grin. "Did we expect anything else?"

"No, but I didn't expect it this soon. How did they know—"

Her troubled question was interrupted by a harsh, shuddering rumble in the bridge beneath them. Almost tumbling out of the side of the wagon, Jessie clutched desperately for the dashboard handhold as the bridge trembled violently again, creaking and groaning.

Alarmed, Ki stood up and peered out over the railing. They were virtually midway across the span, and the North Laramie was a dark, boiling cauldren flowing far below. A phosphorescent stroke of lightning lit the black sky for an instant, and by its white glare, he could see that an old thick spruce had been swept downriver, and had lodged lengthwise against the bridge pilings. Its gnarled branches and roots were gathering other debris—pine and yucca and scrub brush—adding to the weight pressing against the weak, spindly supports.

Ki slapped the reins, sending the team into a protesting gallop. The bridge began twisting, undulating from the mounting force pushing at its pilings, its creaking now growing almost intolerably loud.

There was a wrenching shake as the creaking was drowned out by a sundering roar. The bridge swayed, then dipped, the railings splintering and the deck buckling, dropping apart. The planks fractured in bunches, falling, leaving a gaping hole.

The team plunged through the hole, taking the wagon with it.

Chapter 2

The wagon tilted, upending beneath them. Ki scarcely had time to grip Jessica by one arm before they were hurled, tumbling, out into space and plummeted toward the raging river below. The wagon fell like a stone, shattering in the wreckage of bridge supports and driftwood. But thrown free, Jessica and Ki struck open water on the downriver side, dropping deep underwater and striking submerged rocks.

Dazed and gasping, they surfaced, only to be caught by the surging current. They swam with hard strokes, hampered by their slickers, hardly able to keep from being swept toward a series of sawtoothed boulders through which the river was cascading in deadly, foaming rapids. Half drowned, one hand still clinging to her arm, Ki helped Jessica fight out of the tugging current toward the bank, frantically trying to miss the flotsam of bridge beams, wagon parts, and running gear that were churning around them.

They were less than ten yards from the north bank when a side panel of the wagon reared out of the surface and rammed into Jessica. Ki's grasp was torn loose, and Jessica was thrust, rolling, back into the irresistible hold of the swirling flow. Ki made a lunge for her, but Jessica was already gone, plunging with the side panel toward the bone-smashing, whirling rapids.

Ki dove after her, swimming now with the current in an effort to intercept Jessica. He reached out, missed, stroked, and reached again, fingers tightening on the collar of her slicker. Then he battled one-handedly for the bank again. Taxing his muscles to the utmost, almost losing her again in his frenzied struggle, Ki managed to maneuver them out of the torrent. His boots scraped against stone, and he dug in for a better footing, half climbing, half crawling into a shallow break.

The backwash in this break in the bank created a whirling eddy, and two or three swimming strokes took them to the river's edge. The rain had turned the earth there into a grease-slick ooze, and it was only by clutching at an overhanging limb of a cottonwood that Ki was able at last to drag them both out of the cold rushing water.

Jessica lay on her back, arms flung out, eyes closed, soundless.

Ki knelt and placed his ear to her chest. "You're breathing."

"Of course I'm breathing," Jessie whispered hoarsely, still not moving. "Wait a minute, it's all I can do right now."

A few moments later, Jessie slowly sat up. She coughed, threw up a small quantity of water, then gingerly felt her left shoulder, where the edge of the wagon panel had struck her.

"Are you all right?" Ki asked.

"I think so," she replied, wincing. "It's bruised or maybe wrenched a little, but nothing feels broken."

They rested there for a time, sucking air into their aching

lungs, while the storm battered down and the angry river lapped at their feet. Upriver to their right, the rubbled bridge thrust skeletally toward the dismal sky. Downriver, the rapids were collecting the remains of the wagon and the plump carcasses of the team, along with bridge supports and planks, and much of the same mountainous pile of uprooted brush and trees that had collapsed the span. But the rocks were tougher, withstanding the ravaging pressure.

Jessie was the first to speak. "Gone, Ki, all gone."

"Nothing that can't be replaced."

"I know, Ki, but your weapons..."

"It's not good to become too dependent on weapons. They're merely tools to help in one's task. There are other tools, other ways. Don't worry, the task will be done."

She nodded, biting her lip.

"And our first task," Ki continued affably, standing and offering a hand to Jessica, "must be to find shelter."

Again Jessica nodded, rising and starting with him up the bank to the trail. When he paused on the way to smile encouragingly at her, she managed to respond with a weak smile of her own, sensing that Ki was trying to appear more optimistic than he actually felt. She herself mainly felt anger. As she stumbled over rocks and slipped on the muddy earth, her anger mounted with every step she took, an anger that grew into a grim, purposeful determination to settle the score, barehanded if need be, just as soon as they could reach Eucher Butte.

Angling back upriver toward the bridge, they came to the trail and began following it west again. They trudged slowly, partly from fatigue, partly through caution. The fourth gunman wasn't a threat; he was stuck on the other side of the river and probably thought they were dead. But the unexpected ambush had made them wary, alerting them to the fact that they were known to be traveling this way, at this time. And considering that their only weapons were Ki's *shuriken* and one remaining cartridge in Jessica's derringer, which miraculously had come through entangled in

12

a pocket of her slicker, they both figured that, for now, discretion was a better part of valor.

The trail went along the spine of a low ridge for a while, then came to a plateau overlooking a long stretch of valley ahead. Off to their left, across a weedy field, jutted the angular silhouette of a deserted cabin. From a distance it appeared that some of the roof was missing and the door was sagging on its hinges, but the walls were still standing, and would provide needed protection from the wind and rain. Already Ki could feel a chill seeping through his veins, and though Jessica was uncomplaining, she couldn't keep herself from shivering.

They hastened across the field to the cabin, and went inside; then, propping the door closed, they looked about the dim, musty interior. A crumbling fireplace was built against the far wall, the storm echoing mournfully down its tall chimney. The remnants of a wooden stool and bedframe were cluttering one corner, luckily under a portion of the remaining roof, and when Ki checked the broken pieces, he found them to be rotten and relatively dry.

Swiftly they scraped up the trash and old leaves that littered the floor, piling it all with the broken furniture in the fireplace hearth. Opening his slicker, Ki took from his suit jacket his waterproof box of block matches, and after a few tries, he managed to light a fire.

Satisfied, he stood for a moment with Jessica in front of the warming flames. Then he said, "I'll be back in a short while."

"You're leaving? No, Ki, not without me—"

"Stay here, Jessie, and get dry. After that dunking you took, you'd risk catching pneumonia if you went out again."

"And you couldn't, too? Ki, where are you going?"

Ki, already at the door, merely answered with a soft, knowing smile. Then, closing the door behind him, he stepped out into the cold, rain-lashing storm. The first task was done; now for the second.

He set off in a steady run back toward the river. It distressed him to leave Jessica filled with questions and doubts; but to have explained, he felt, would have resulted either in her refusing to let him go, or her insisting on coming along. It would have taken too long to persuade her otherwise, and time was of the essence. Alone, he could make better time. Indeed, if he'd been alone before, he wouldn't have left the river; only the priority of finding shelter for Jessica had compelled him to act as he had.

Arriving at the ruined bridge, he angled downriver, veering down the bank and sprinting along the water's edge to the rapids. The turbulent river was swirling against the rocks, spuming over the haphazard dam of debris that was trapped, higher and thicker than ever, like bits of food between the teeth of a giant. Without hesitating, Ki ripped off his slicker, suit jacket, and Wellington boots, and dove in.

The rampaging current carried him toward the nearer of the two channels that formed a fork on either side of the jutting boulders. Swimming furiously, he propelled himself toward the middle of the river, and a moment later he was flung violently against the choking mound of debris. The shock of his impact dislodged one of the dead Morgans, which squeezed between the rocks and was carried away.

Frigid hands clawing for a hold, Ki lifted himself out of the water and onto the rough, scrubby branches of a yellow pine. Balancing gingerly, testing for weight and shifting before each step, he carefully eased among the debris and rocks, poking deep and clearing away, searching to recover what might remain of theirs.

Time, precious time. If he'd been able to begin his hunt earlier, when the shattered wagon had first washed up against the rocks, he'd have had a better chance of finding things. If he'd waited much longer than he had, it would have been hopeless. Every minute, the raging tide was adding new debris, pushing forward what was there already, covering over the old and grinding it up, then prying it loose and sending it swirling away, lost forever.

He spent almost an hour in his search, digging with his hands and clinging precariously with his feet. His weapons were gone. Those made of wood, like his bows and arrows and *nunchaku* sticks, had undoubtedly floated away immediately. Those of metal, like his *sai* swords and studded mail gloves, simply had sunk to the bottom. And his explosive devices would be beyond use, even if he discovered any—which he didn't.

But with a sigh of relief, Ki managed to locate Jessica's bulky trunk. Its top was crushed and one side was stove in, and its Excelsior lock was snapped open and twisted awry. Its two hefty leather straps still held it closed, however, though tree roots were wedged between them and the lid, making it difficult to haul from the debris.

At the other end of the rapids, where the carcass of the second Morgan remained hooked to the harness, Ki discovered his own Bellows case. This took even greater effort to extract, caught as it was in the venturi of two boulders, and firmly held underwater by the leaden foreleg of the dead horse. Launching himself into the water, Ki prodded and shoved and wrenched, struggling to keep from being sucked through the geysering vortex between the boulders. For a seemingly endless time, the case refused to budge, only the fact that it was made of impervious "alligator keratol" saving it from breaking apart in Ki's levering tug-of-war with the rocks. Stubbornly Ki kept working, determined to reclaim the case, which not only contained a change of clothing, but his prized multipocket vest and an emergency assortment of smaller weapons—throwing daggers, spare *shuriken*, and the like.

At last he maneuvered his case free. Thrusting it and himself out of the water, he carried it across to where he'd upended Jessica's trunk to drain, at the edge of the debris closest to the bank. Then, taking a deep breath and an iron grip on the case, he slid back into the river and began an agonizing one-handed crawl toward the shore. He fought the current, counting each off-balance stroke in his mind, savoring each yard he gained. Grabbing at slick tufts of grass growing along the bank, he tossed the sodden case up onto the ground.

Again, hesitating only long enough to fill his lungs, Ki dove back to the rapids to retrieve the trunk. It was larger and heavier than his case, weighing him down like a waterlogged anchor as he hugged it with his left hand and braced himself against the river's brutal rush.

The current pummeled him, tossing him into a dangerous tangent. Despite himself, despite his years of training and experience, a sensation of dread seeped through Ki as he forged again toward the bank. He'd made a mistake, a fatal error, tackling too great and awkward a load this time, and he was going to be swept away and drowned. He forced down his panic, calling on the last of his inner resources to strain forward, wrestling with the pitching, sinking trunk. He could not die this way, it would not happen, it was not a true thing.

God, but it was, it was. His chest was throbbing, aching, and there was a ringing in his ears, and for an instant he thought the feel of stone and sediment under his feet was a hallucination. Ki clawed onwards, knowing that if it was a mirage, it really didn't make any difference. It was all over but the swallowing.

Kicking, frantic to relieve the pressure in his lungs, he reached the shallows, head reeling and stomach knotting with convulsions. Water boiled against his thighs as he straightened, choking and gagging, and shoved the trunk the last few feet to the bank. Wading, he dragged it to the safety of a sloping ledge and slumped beside it. His strength was sapped. He lay there, momentarily helpless, while with wracking coughs he dispelled muddy river water from his lungs.

When he felt somewhat recovered, Ki carted the trunk up to where he'd dumped the case, and tilted both on end to drain them. Slowly he collected his jacket, slicker, and boots, and after dressing he waited a bit longer, recouping

16

more of his flagging energy. Then, balancing the cumbersome trunk on his back, holding it steady with one hand, he picked up the case in his other hand and set off up the bank toward the trail.

Chapter 3

Ki's return to the cabin was steady but sluggish, the storm flailing about him. Gradually the wind lowered, and in time the rain lessened into a chilling drizzle. The overcast parted, drifting southward, but now the sky was dark with late evening. Stars began to glimmer here and there, and a pale quarter moon was a blurry crescent in the blue-black dome surrounding it.

Ki savored the washed freshness of the crisp evening breeze. He made little effort to avoid detection, walking openly along the center strip of the trail, bending low with the weight of his load, moving by sheer reflex. If he was attacked now, he doubted he had enough strength left to fight, and he was becoming so numbed with exhaustion that he was almost past the point of caring.

Eventually he reached the field, and saw smoke spiraling from the chimney of the cabin. Heartened, he quickened his pace. When he arrived, he put down his case long enough to open the door, then stepped inside.

The interior was bathed in a ruddy glow from the fireplace blaze. Jessica stood with her back to the fire, steam wisping from her tweed riding jacket and skirt, her blonde hair plastered wetly to her head. When she saw Ki enter, she rushed forward to help him, her green eyes widening with relief and surprise.

"Ki! How on earth did you—"

"Never mind how," Ki gasped, dropping her trunk and the case next to the hearth. "It needed to be done, and it was."

"No, it didn't. You said yourself everything was replaceable."

"So I first thought. Then I remembered your father's book."

Jessica paused, nodding thoughtfully. "You're right, Ki, I'd brought it along. But it was still a horrid chance for you to take, and I'm not sure it was worth the risk of losing you as well."

"Ah, but you didn't, Jessie. I'm here, the book is here, and a lot of other things are here that we'd better get to drying."

"And one of those things is you," Jessica said pointedly. "I'll unpack, it's the least I can do, while you shuck some of those sopping wet clothes and rest by the fire. And, Ki?"

"Yes?"

"Thank you."

Ki smiled wearily in acknowledgement, and gladly accepted her suggestion. He stripped off his slicker, suit jacket, and black ankle-high boots again, adding to them now his socks, sky-blue shirt, and string tie, leaving himself clad only in his drenched trousers.

He settled comfortably, cross-legged, before the crackling fire, and started breathing in through his nose and out through his mouth. When he'd slowed his inhalation/exhalation cycle to ten breaths a minute, he cupped his right ear with the palm of his left hand, and concentrated on one thought: relaxation. After five minutes, he switched to the other hand and ear. After another five, he crossed his arms and covered both ears, still breathing inaudibly, his tongue adhering to the roof of his mouth. And in that position he remained.

Meanwhile, Jessie was busily emptying his case. She laid out his denim jeans, collarless shirt, rope-soled cloth slippers, and brown leather vest near the hearth and wiped and cleaned his weapons with the hem of her skirt. Then she arranged the case so that it too would dry. Nothing, she was relieved to find, appeared ruined.

Then she turned to her trunk. Opening it, she realized bleakly that it was beyond salvation and would have to be replaced. Blessedly, it had stayed together enough to protect the contents. Most of her extra clothes were ruined, but her wide brown belt was fine, and there wasn't much damage that could be done to her well-worn jeans and matching denim jacket—except maybe to shrink some more, and they already fit her as snugly as a second skin.

Resting on the trunk's linen-lined set-up tray was her custom .38 Colt revolver, still in its waxed holster, along with a gun-cleaning kit, a cut-crystal perfume atomizer, and a few other feminine trinkets. These she set aside, lifting the tray's bottom, which acted as the lid of a second compartment underneath. She removed a letter and a black calf-skin-bound pocket notebook, silently thanking Ki again for having endangered his life to recover them.

Taking the letter and book to the hearth, she propped them up to dry. Then, on second thought, she picked up the letter again to see if the soaking had made it illegible. The notebook worried her less; she knew its entries were in india ink, having frequently studied the pages of names, dates, and places since her father, the author of the notebook's contents, had died, leaving it in a hidden compartment of his old rolltop desk.

The letter was on a single sheet of tablet paper, and though some of its writing was smeared a little, it had been protected by the envelope. Postmarked six weeks ago at

Eucher Butte, it had been penned with exquisite script in stilted, formal language:

To Whom It May Concern:

This is to inform you that my husband, Uriah, recently passed away. I must mention this grievous tragedy in detail for two reasons, one being the peculiar nature of his death, and the other being the resultant inability to continue business relations as contracted between the Flying W and the Circle Star.

My husband, a star rider all of his life, nevertheless was found by our foreman after apparently having fallen from his horse and been dragged a considerable distance. When I questioned this and insisted on a fuller investigation, I was subsequently informed by Sheriff Quincy Oakes that inspection revealed a massive blow inflicted to the forehead, and other indications that this injury had not been inflicted by a horse, but had caused death before dragging took place. Unfortunately, as suspicious as this might sound, I have been unable to gain further help or to alter the verdict of accidental death.

I suspect my husband met his untimely demise through foul play. Shortly before his supposed accident, he turned down an offer to sell the Flying W to Captain Guthried Ryker, owner of the nearby Block-Two-Dot ranch. Shortly afterwards, I was approached by this same man. To be perfectly candid, I am afraid I hold a low opinion of Captain Ryker's basic nature, in spite of his outwardly civilized manner, and cannot but wonder if he felt that his purchase would be easier to negotiate with a widow.

I am adamantly opposed to selling, particularly to Captain Ryker. I believe I should warn you, however, that soon I may be forced to put the ranch up for auction. My husband brought me here from Boston just a few years ago, and I know little about ranching.

Rustlers have been raiding our stock. I have been required to withdraw heavily from our savings, and face having to borrow funds to operate. If matters continue as they have, we will surely be unable to meet the quota of cattle we agreed to supply the Circle Star by this coming autumn.

I have no proof, and you could very well regard me as a silly and incompetent hysteric. Yet I am convinced that my late husband and I have been the victims of an unscrupulous plot to wrest ownership of our ranch. I beg your indulgence and understanding, and remain

Y'r m'st ob'd'nt s'rv'nt,
(Mrs.) Amabelle Pons Waldemar

"I certainly don't think you're silly or crazy, Mrs. Waldemar," Jessica sighed aloud, spreading the letter back out on the hearth.

She crossed to her slicker and took out her derringer, then went to her trunk and unwrapped the gun-cleaning kit. All the while she mulled over the letter, pondering how it fit with other facts she knew. Closing the lid of the trunk, she sat down on it and began drying and lubricating the derringer, then hesitated, frowning as she glanced over to where Ki was still squatting motionless.

"Ki, how did Ryker know we were coming?"

"Your supper with Governor Hoyt," Ki murmured, unmoving.

"Of course," Jessie said, mostly to herself. Finishing with the derringer, she picked up her revolver and started to clean it, her mind shaping small links into a pattern, as a child might fashion a delicate pine-needle chain. Her eyes flashed a peculiar greenish shade, the hue of an iceberg's edge when salt water washed it. Her father would have said she was in one of her "damned moods."

Amabelle Waldemar's letter, which had started it all, had been addressed to the general offices of the huge Starbuck cattle operation in Texas, headquartered at the sprawling Circle Star ranch. Initially it was treated the same as the many other missives received every day, and was transferred to the section that handled sales and purchases for routine response. On the surface, it *was* routine. Starbuck contracted with hundreds of small, under-financed ranches to supply beef for the burgeoning markets in America and Europe, and a certain percentage of failures and bankruptcies were expected.

In the case of Waldemars' Flying W, it was one of a half-dozen borderline ranches in the area, which the Circle Star had helped to arrange into a loose sort of cooperative. Banding together allowed the ranches to operate as effectively as larger spreads, but the Circle Star's motives were not entirely altruistic, for it also guaranteed a reasonably steady source of meat.

The previous October, the Circle Star had been notified that the Block-Two-Dot ranch had been sold and was dropping out of the co-op. Starbuck field men, going there to try renegotiating the deal, reported back that they'd been tossed off the property at gunpoint. At the time, neither this nor the name of the new owner sparked any alarm. Then Amabelle Waldemar's letter arrived. A sharp-witted clerk, perceiving that an anguished plea for help was implied in the message, and remembering the strange incident at the Block-Two-Dot, sent the letter and a memo explaining the connection on to his superiors for review.

It didn't take long for Jessica to get the letter—after all, the Starbuck buck stopped with her. Reading it and the memo, the name of the Block-Two-Dot's owner struck her as sounding familiar, and she then began leafing through the pages of the little black book.

Guthried Ryker was listed in it.

Another connection was now forged, one far more sinister than the lowly clerk could have imagined. Contained within the notebook's leather covers was a ledger detailing the names and activities of a vicious international ring intent upon gaining control of America's business and political establishment. Jessica's father had started compiling the information while in the Orient, during his first meager years of building what would ultimately become the Starbuck business empire, and had scrupulously kept the book up to date ever since. In his subsequent battles with this criminal conspiracy, his wife was killed while Jessica was still a baby. Eventually he too was murdered; though, by then, Jessica was a young woman, old enough to know and understand his persistent fight.

Vowing revenge, and aided by Ki and her wealthy inheritance, Jessica continued her father's war against the insidious network of graft and corruption—against the traitorous businessmen, lawmen, politicians, and outright crooks who'd sold out America to this merciless cabal that had slaughtered her parents. Guthried Ryker was one of them.

The entry stated that Ryker, Guthried Hannibal, aged forty-seven, had been born to a socially prominent family in Philadelphia. He was well educated, with no military service—putting the lie to his aggrandizing title of "Captain." He was unmarried, and a frequenter of prostitutes who specialized in whips and ropes. Currently he was the figurehead president of Acme Packers & Purveyors, a front company for the ring, which operated out of the Chicago stockyards.

Evidently, Ryker was quite the city-slick bastard...

And at the moment, as Jessica sat on her broken trunk, rubbing whale oil on her revolver, she couldn't help wondering why the devil Ryker had chosen to move to Eucher Butte. She could envision the kind of man he was: ambitious, greedy, devious, with a streak of cruelty just beneath his sophisticated facade. He would likely enjoy the role of cattle baron, but she couldn't figure how he hoped to attain that by owning such piddling ranches as the Block-Two-Dot and the Waldemars' Flying W. Nor could Jessica see him running them. If the report was accurate, and she'd no reason to doubt it, Guthried Ryker had never roped, branded, or castrated a calf; had probably never, in fact, stepped in cow dung. He was the type who'd stay comfortably away and hire lesser men to do his dirty work for him.

Dirty work like the ambush that had been laid for Ki and herself.

The surprise attack at the bridge still puzzled her. Ki had answered the *how* behind it: Ryker had undoubtedly heard they were coming, thanks to John W. Hoyt, territorial governor of Wyoming. Hoyt had greeted Jessica and Ki in Cheyenne, admitting that he'd learned of their arrival from the Wichita stationmaster, who'd recognized Jessica when they'd boarded the Union Pacific there, and had wired ahead for red-carpet service, thinking he was doing her a service.

Hoyt had insisted that *the* Starbuck of *the* Starbuck empire dine with him at the capital. On trips like this, Jessica preferred to keep a low profile, but there hadn't been any way to decline his offer graciously. She'd been politely vague about their destination, even though she knew the governor to be an honorable man beyond reproach. Nor did she believe he'd purposely tipped off Ryker—except perhaps in the same respect as the stationmaster had, by innocently requesting other important personages to host her royally wherever she went. And certainly, as president of a Chicago packing company, Ryker was the most—probably the only—person of any note around Eucher Butte. On the other hand, the news could just as easily have been sent by an eager reporter or political flunky keeping tabs on the governor's doings. Whatever, the dinner's high visibility had resulted in warning Ryker, giving him plenty of time to arrange an appropriate welcome...

But that still failed to solve the *why* of it. Obviously, Ryker had deduced that he was the reason for their trip, and had figured to kill them before they could threaten his schemes. Jessica didn't know what those schemes might be, yet for Ryker to have tried such a drastic act as that ambush convinced her he was after more than merely grabbing the Flying W. No matter what his motives, one fact was clear: their journey to Eucher Butte was already proving to be complicated and dangerous, far more than their original purpose of helping Amabelle Waldemar would have led them to believe.

"I hate to admit it, Ki," Jessica said, setting her revolver aside and smoothing her skirt, "but Ryker has got me baffled."

Ki said nothing.

"I mean, what's he up to?" she continued. "The region's pretty remote, lacking mining potential and only fair for grazing, and the only rumors of a possible new rail line are about the Chicago & Northwestern laying track way to the north. What do you think?"

Ki still did not respond.

Jessica looked carefully at Ki, wondering if something was wrong with him. He remained quiet and motionless in his cross-legged, cross-armed position—a position she knew he used for more than simple relaxation. As Ki had often told her, it was a position he practiced for fifteen or twenty minutes almost daily, as an exercise to strengthen what he termed his "intrinsic energy," that inner concentrating force which permeated most Asian martial-arts systems, and which was the underlying basis of his own power and agility.

No, nothing seemed to be wrong. In fact, as Jessica started toward him to check, Ki appeared to look superbly healthy. With his lithe-muscled naked back, his bronzed bare arms, and his mane of blue-black hair cascading around his corded shoulders, he resembled something like a pagan earth god, virile and primally desirable.

Reaching Ki, Jessica felt her breasts begin to tingle perversely, and she told herself to be a good girl. Ki was out of bounds, just as she was for him. It wasn't because he worked for her; Ki may have been on a different social level, but so had been many of her lovers. And it wasn't because he would have rebuffed her seduction; though unspoken, she was aware of how greatly he cared for her. Rather, it was because they were as brother and sister, two halves of a partnership equal and compatible. To have surrendered to a moment of physical bliss would have ruptured forever that deeper, more fundamental bond of admiration, trust, and affection that they held for each other.

She touched him lightly. "Ki?" she whispered.

Ki did not answer. He was sound asleep.

Chapter 4

The night passed without incident.

Jessica and Ki awakened just before daybreak, to find that the residue of the storm had blown itself away, wheeling south into Colorado. But the fire had long since burned out, and the gray false dawn was cold, adding impetus to their movements as they hurriedly changed their clothes and left the cabin for Eucher Butte.

In the flush of a serene, fiery dawn, they began their long hike down the trail. Jessica was now in her figure-squeezing denim jeans and jacket, her derringer concealed behind the wide square buckle of her belt, her custom .38 holstered at her thigh, her notebook safely hidden inside her silk blouse, pressing against her flat belly under the swell of her firm, unbound breasts. Ki too was wearing jeans, along with his cotton-twill shirt and moccasin-like slippers, the weapons he'd salvaged from his case now hidden on his body and in the many pockets of his worn leather vest.

They reached Eucher Butte with the noon sun overhead, the Wyoming sky a soft powder-blue enamel, warm and benevolent.

The town swelled like a festering sore near the banks of the North Laramie, sprawling in the same pattern as a thousand other small cow towns, with an outscatter of corrals and sheds at one end, and a rutted main street leading to a cluster of frame houses at the other.

Walking along, Jessica and Ki passed a livery stable and yard, a funeral home, a gunsmith, and an imposing saloon with the name THUNDERMUG painted on its etched-glass windows. Directly across from the saloon was a combination barbershop and bath house, and a tucked-away restaurant with no name at all. Farther on could be seen a bootmaker, a general store and feedlot, and a false-fronted three-story hotel called the GRAND CONTINENTAL, with most of its ground floor taken up by a bank. Flanking the hotel was a telegraph and post office, and a bleak stone building with a weathered sign over its door reading ALBANY CO. SHERIFF. Buckboards and wagons were almost as prevalent as horses, and the boardwalks were crowded for this time of day, sure signs that, come evening, a lot of merry hurrahing would break loose in the gaming rooms and crib parlors of the large, obviously profitable saloon.

They went as far as the restaurant, where they ordered the first decent meal they'd had since yesterday morning. While eating, Jessica thought that probably Eucher Butte wasn't too awful a place—it merely seemed that way. It was wild, typical of the territory and the breed infesting it, no worse than other small cattle towns and maybe a little better. She doubted they'd get much cooperation here; likely the townsfolk wouldn't be partial to strangers poking their noses in local affairs, especially now that Ryker, forewarned, had had a chance to cover himself and spread a bunch of horse manure around. But it would furnish their more immediate needs, and from that point of view, Eucher Butte was quite satisfactory.

Leaving the restaurant, Ki said, "No telling what Ryker has in mind, Jessie, and I'd hate for him to catch you with empty pistols. Let me go buy you some fresh ammunition. Then, if you want, I'll hire a horse and ride back to the cabin to collect our luggage."

"It's liable to be all stolen by now."

Ki shrugged. "No great loss," he replied, adding with a sly grin, "besides, if any thief looked finer in your tweed outfit than you do, I'd say you ought to let him keep it."

Jessica laughed. "I would, gladly. Better yet, Ki, see if you can find some kid who'd fetch it for you, and ask directions to the Flying W. If there's time, we'll ride out there today. If not, we'll stay over at the hotel and leave early tomorrow."

"Good idea. Then where will I meet you?"

"At the sheriff's, I imagine."

"You're going to report the ambush?"

"I might. Won't know till I size up the man," Jessica said, "and get a feel as to which side of the ambush he'd have been fighting on."

They parted, and Jessica strode along the boardwalk to the sheriff's office. Even before opening the door, she could hear an angry voice shouting inside. Entering, she faced a fat, fiftyish man sitting tilted in a swivel chair, and the back of a younger man standing with his fists clenched on top of the littered desk between them.

"Haul your ass out and put a stop to it, Quince!" the younger man was yelling. "My crew's threatening to quit, and after that raid the night 'fore last, when Rasmussen got shot dead and three others got winged, I can't rightly blame 'em if they skedaddled. Just like all my goddamned rustled cows you can't find went and skedaddled."

"Easy, Daryl, a lady's present," the fat man growled, seeing Jessica and straightening in his chair. "Yes, ma'am?"

"Are you Sheriff Oakes?"

"Deputy Sheriff, yes," the fat man answered, preening one end of the graying mustache that drooped around his pudgy mouth and jowls. A tobacco dribble stained his vest next to his tarnished star. "Something I can do for you, ma'am?"

"Maybe the same thing you can do for him," Jessica answered, indicating the other man with a glancing nod.

She judged the man, who'd now turned toward her, to be about thirty, six foot one or two, maybe two hundred pounds, with a hardness that didn't come from riding a brass rail. Tousled hair the shade of dressed harness leather, brushed long under a wide-brimmed, flat-crowned Kansas hat. Big beak of a nose and an anvil for a chin. Magnetic eyes that appraised her squarely. His frayed range clothes were sweaty and dirty, and the Remington .44-40 stuck in his belt was a relic with cracked grips, but this was no saddle tramp; he was a man used to giving orders and having them obeyed. She liked him immediately.

Regarding Deputy Oakes again, she continued, "You can track down and arrest these rustlers and killers hereabouts, that's what you can do. But I gather you haven't been much good at it."

Stung, the deputy frowned, puffing his cheeks. "Can't say I place you, ma'am. Forgive me if I ask just who you are, and if you've got any special interest in our local problems."

"I most certainly have," Jessica retorted archly. "My name's Starbuck, Miss Jessica Starbuck, and I've got a considerable interest in the Flying W." Which, in a manner of speaking, was true enough.

She left it at that, deciding not to mention the ambush. Even if Deputy Oakes acted on it, she figured he wouldn't be able to do or prove much; Ryker was too clever not to have removed his dead gunmen and cleaned up any other evidence that might incriminate him. And the deputy didn't look like the sort who'd bust a gut investigating; he looked like he'd been in that swivel chair a mighty long time, and was tired of hearing about trouble.

Jessica's name seemed to spark recognition in the other man, but if Deputy Oakes realized who she was, he didn't show it.

"Poor widder Waldemar, a shame, a shame," the deputy murmured, then eyed Jessica glumly. "I'm not surprised she's sold to an outsider, it's a terrible lot for her to try running all by her lonesome. But like I was about to tell Mr. Melville here, I've been worn to a frazzle chasing one blind lead after another."

"Well, if you won't do more'n you have," Melville snapped, "then I reckon us ranchers will have to protect ourselves."

Oakes leaned back again, shifting uncomfortably. "It's not that I won't, Daryl, it's that all I've got is me and my night man. Sure's I ride out to your spread, the coyotes are hitting the Double Diamond. I ride there, and they strike Leach's Lazy L."

"As Miss Starbuck said, Quince, track them down."

"Don't think I haven't tried. But once off the flatlands, we lose them up in the rock canyons. Can't even get a line on where the cattle's being sold, either, no sign of any of your herds showing up anywhere in the territory. It's just like the mountains opened up and swallowed them whole, and I tell you, it's got me buffaloed."

"Well, I guess that means me and the others will have to form a vigilante committee," Melville said, glaring as he leaned over the desk again. "I know it's illegal, but we're fed up with losing our men and cattle."

Deputy Oakes brooded, as if considering the ultimatum. "Daryl," he finally said, "I'll ask you not to go off half cocked. Let me wire my boss in Laramie to send some more deputies. I'll scatter them around, and we're sure to get a lead on where the rustlers are rat-holed. You tell that to the others, will you?"

"I'll try," Melville replied. "They might not listen."

"Make them listen. Letting your crews run around with itchy trigger fingers can only lead to worse trouble, not less. I mean this for your own good. I'd really regret having to arrest you or any of your men for taking the law into your own hands."

"All right, Quince, I'll string along with you awhile

longer." Straightening, Melville started for the door. He paused, hand on the knob, to add, "But things have to change around here, and fast."

"They will, Daryl," Deputy Oakes replied with an earnest heartiness. "You've got my word. You can count on it."

Melville nodded and opened the door, then hesitated again to look at Jessica. "Coming, Miss Starbuck?"

It was less a question than a command, and normally such a tone would have provoked Jessica. But she had no more to say to Deputy Oakes, and plenty to ask Daryl Melville. Besides, she was interested in knowing why he'd raised his eyebrows when he heard her name. So, with a parting smile to the deputy, she went out the door that Melville was holding open for her.

Before she could utter a word, Melville started angling across the street, his long swift strides hard for her to follow.

"Where are you going so fast?" she asked.

"To get my father," he said, slowing so she could catch up. His onyx eyes were flashing more irately than ever. "He's over in the Thundermug, half swacked by now. The damn dog-bleeding crooks."

"Who?"

"Halford and Kendrick, bartender and gambler, the owners of the dive. If one doesn't rob you, the other one will. Say, by any chance would you be related to the Starbucks in Texas?"

"Yes. Why?"

"I'm one of the ranchers in the Circle Star co-op."

"Oh? Which one?"

"Spraddled M. M for Melville." Reaching the boardwalk on the opposite side of the street, he stopped and smiled at Jessica. "Daryl Melville. And my father, Tobias, of course; he started it after driving cattle up from Texas back in the early seventies."

"You sound proud of it."

"Dirt-proud, mostly, but it's home," he responded wryly, and gestured down the street, where the trail continued west to Garrett. "There's a fork in the road a fair piece from

33

here, that goes to five spreads back in the slopes, including ours and the Flying W. There ain't none of us but hasn't fought everything Mother Nature has to throw, and we were winning until this thieving and murdering came along. Hate to say it, but you rode into a range that's raring to explode."

"I've done that before," Jessica said quietly.

"I admire your spunk," he said, starting up the boardwalk again, "but it's too bad you didn't know this before buying out Mrs. Waldemar."

"I haven't. My only interest is to protect the investment Starbuck has in her herd. In all your herds, if possible. But are you ranchers truly serious about forming a vigilante committee?"

Melville gave a laugh, short and bitter. "I was pure bluffing. The big ranchers don't need to, they've got their own guards. And the smaller ranchers are afraid that to fight back would goad the rustlers into wiping them out, man, woman, and child. So all they're willing to do is stand pat like sheep, doing nothing 'cept bleat and leak in their pants, if you'll pardon the expression, Miss Starbuck."

"Jessie."

"All right, but only if you call me Daryl. And don't get me wrong, but I can't see how you hope to help the lady, Jessie."

"First, by riding out there this afternoon for a talk."

"Won't make it before dark, I'm afraid, and the Flying W isn't much set up for overnight guests. Or are you already expected?"

"Not especially, no. I'd better wait till tomorrow morning."

"Well, you can leave word with her crew that you're coming," he said caustically, thumbing toward a knot of horses tied in front of the saloon. "Crews are like mavericks, they have to be taught who's boss and be ridden on short rein. Otherwise they run wild."

Melville moved through the batwings without holding them open for Jessie; it never dawned on him that a rowdy saloon would be a place she'd visit. She followed anyway,

34

her curiosity piqued by his comment about the Flying W crew, and stood unobtrusively along the wall by the entrance. The Thundermug was aptly named, she thought.

Melville was brushing between the mostly empty tables, thrusting toward the card tables and chuckaluck layout clustered near the rear. It was far too early for much action in the saloon, not even any drink-caging bar girls around yet, and what patrons there were seemed more interested in boozing than gambling. Only a small group of players and kibitzers were gathered at a single smoke-obscured card table, and from what Jessica could see of it, there didn't appear to be any high-stakes excitement going on.

The drinkers were mainly in two separate clumps at the shiny mahogany bar that stretched along one wall. The nearer men were sullenly quiet, a ferret-eyed watchfulness on their lanky, stubbled faces, a challenging bravado to their display of bristling weapons. The other bunch were nondescript cowpunchers, wearing pistols out of habit, the tools of their trade the rope and ring and branding iron. It was from them that Jessica heard the dull roar of talking and laughing, the clink of glasses and bottles.

Behind the bar, two white-aproned tenders were busily pouring. Brackets and chandeliers reflected in the polished backbar mirrors, and gleamed against the huge portrait of a buxom reclining nude. Seated on a high stool next to the nude, presiding over it all, was a frog of a fellow with slicked-down balding hair and a handlebar mustache, a nugget chain looped across a flowered vest, a torpedo cigar clenched in his gold-capped teeth.

He, Jessie surmised, would be Halford, one of the owners. And the boys happily lapping up his rotgut would be Mrs. Waldemar's crew. Melville was right—they were going to have to learn some loyalty and earn their keep. Before Jessica or anyone else would have a prayer to saving the Flying W, those men would have to be out there riding, and riding with everything they had. And the more Jessica looked at them and considered their failings, the more incensed she became.

Finally, beyond endurance, Jessie strode up to the crew. "Drink hearty," she snapped in a cold, cutting voice. "Because this'll be the last drink you'll have on the Flying W payroll."

Startled heads turned. A hush fell over the bar.

Then one of the men chuckled cynically. "Aw, hell, it's only a female." He was a bowlegged, weatherbeaten man with a nut-shaped head of narrow, sly features; he was older than the others, who were rawboned youths with devil-may-care in their eyes. "Don't pay her no mind, boys, you know how women go on the prod."

Jessica eyed him sharply. "You must be the foreman."

"Uh-huh. Nealon's the name, but you can call me Lloyd."

"I call you a bum."

"What?" He reared back, glowering. "Just who d'you think you are, comin' in here where you don't belong, pesterin' and insultin' us?"

"I'm Starbuck," she said flatly. "By contract, I own the beef you're not herding. Mrs. Waldemar wrote that she had problems, and now I can sure understand why, with a slob like you rodding a pack of lazy, elbow-bending drunks."

The others were staring dumbfounded, but Nealon was growing crimson, champing at the bit. "Okay, sweets, enough of your gag."

"It's no gag. And if you think it is, Nealon, you're dumber than you're acting already." She stepped closer, surveying the crew, her hands in fists on her hips. "Now open your ears, because I'm going to say this only once. I've come a long way to help the Flying W, and I don't have the time or patience to fool around. I'm going to be out there early tomorrow morning, and any of you who aren't up and out working, and working hard, will be fired."

A babbling broke out among the crew—all except for Nealon, who was now the one to stare gawking, silent and stupified.

Before they could collect their wits, Jessie pivoted to stalk away. And two things happened, almost simultaneously. Ki walked through the batwings and, seeing her, started across. And from the card table rose an infuriated bellow: "You skunk, Kendrick, I oughta break every bone in your body with my bare hands!"

"Lay a finger on me and I'll kill you!" a second voice shouted almost as loudly. "I run a friendly, honest game here, and your old man sat in of his own free will. Now get him and get out!"

Jessie and Ki, along with most everybody at the bar, headed toward the back, joining the watchers around the table. Cards and chips were scattered all over. Two players were seated with their eyes wide, mouths shut, hands flat on the green felt—the best position to hold when a game was in dispute. A third player was a bull-bodied, whiskery brute who was obviously enjoying the ruckus and was feeling immune, lounging back in his chair with a contemptuous smirk pasted on his brutal, scarred face.

Slumped in a fourth chair, his head resting on the table, was a white-haired elderly man. Tobias Melville, Jessie assumed. His son Daryl was towering behind him, face gnarled with rage and nearly as red as Nealon's had been. Across from them, standing where his chair had tipped over, was the fifth player, a squat, plumpish man with a cherubic face and pouty lips, garbed in a black cutaway coat, ruffled shirt, string tie, and a rakishly tilted green Keevil hat.

As Jessie and Ki approached, Melville was snarling at him, "Sure, you run it friendly and honest, all right. About as friendly as a rattler, Kendrick, and you give a man just about as much chance."

"I won't take no more of this," the gambler warned.

"You'll take it," Melville raged heedlessly, one hand gripping his father's lax shoulder. "You've been taking everything else from us for months now, when you know we can't pay, only go deeper into debt to you. You and Halford have been addling him with whiskey till he can't tell an ace from a queen. Just look what you've done to him!"

"Yeah, the old fool's passed out cold," the smirking

37

player cut in snidely. The other players stayed quiet and still, unwilling to intrude. "Tell you what, Melville, I'll help you. I'll help you carry him out and dump him in the closest horse trough."

The man snickered at his own joke. He was big enough to get away with it, taller than Melville and heftier by a good ten pounds. But Melville was beyond caution now, and he focused all his pent-up fury on the sneering giant, his voice like the edge of a scythe.

"Shut your mouth, Volpes, before I shut it for you. I've had it with you too, just like the other ranchers have had it. We're out there working, trying to live decent, but for some reason all you can think to do is sneer and bully like the king of the shitpile."

Volpes rose swinging.

An uppercutting haymaker crunched against Melville's jaw with a meaty impact, sending him reeling off balance. Wincing with pain, Melville shook his head to clear it, falling back a pace to regain his footing, as Volpes confidently charged to polish him off.

Melville ducked the onrushing roundhouse fist, dancing aside and striking back with a jolting right-left to Volpes's stomach and heart. The attack caught Volpes surprised and unguarded, but he moved in undaunted, hammering with abandon. Melville shifted and feinted, evading the blows, stabbing two lefts to Volpes's face so fast that one had scarcely hit before the other had landed.

Then a roundhouse knuckler cracked alongside Melville's cheek, momentarily stunning him. Before he could recover, Volpes got an arm around him and smashed him twice in the face with stiff, short-range punches. Melville butted him hard, breaking free, and launched another one-two combination. His left opened a gash over Volpes's eye, the right flattened the bridge of his nose. Volpes staggered, spurting blood from his nostrils, and the customers yelled.

And the gambler went for a belly-gun. Or at least it appeared that way, Kendrick barking an oath and darting

38

his hand inside his coat, where a stubby-barreled weapon would be hidden in a shoulder holster.

Before Kendrick could produce whatever he was after, Ki took a step forward, his arm blurring up and out. A throwing dagger winked across the table. Kendrick choked on his oath, his hand still dipped inside his coat, and stared down at the jutting hilt of the knife, which had sliced through his coat pocket, skinning his ribs.

"The next will be closer," Ki called, smiling.

Kendrick grinned weakly and removed his hand.

The fighters traded blows, Volpes the stronger and cruelly effective, and Melville the faster and angrily impervious. Ignoring the battering jabs and chops, Melville returned rights and lefts until he'd wiped Volpes's smirk off his face, and sealed up the eye with the cut over it. Volpes dove, grappling, to wrap him in another crushing hug, but this time Melville was prepared, catching Volpes by the beard and jerking his face downward, mashing Volpes's already broken nose against his rising right knee. Pushing Volpes away then, Melville hit him a half-dozen more times in both eyes. Like a blundering, blind bear, Volpes tried to slug back, but Melville went under the swings and pummeled him in the belly and face, driving Volpes against the table, overturning it, punching him the length of the saloon and pinning him against the bar. Dazed and bleeding, Volpes sagged to his knees, bewildered by the unleashed fury of Melville's assault.

Melville hauled Volpes to his feet, while the crowd closed in around them, baying for the finishing blow. They weren't disappointed. Melville brought his right fist up from somewhere down around his boots. It hit Volpes's chin with the sound heard in a slaughterhouse, when a steer was brained with a maul. Volpes arched backward and slid five feet along the sawdust-covered planks, coming to rest when his head struck a brass spittoon. He didn't get up.

Melville stood catching his breath, looking moodily down at Volpes. Then, turning, he thrust through the congratulatory throng to where his father sprawled snoring on the floor, the old man having fallen there when the table overturned. Jessica and Ki followed, and Ki helped Melville pick up his father and dust him off.

Kendrick, who was righting the table, paused to give the two men a murderous glare. "From now on, you're both barred from here."

Melville, misunderstanding, snapped, "That's dandy by me. I've been trying long enough to stop Dad from coming in this snakepit."

"Oh, Toby's welcome anytime. I mean you—and *him*."

Melville regarded Ki and then the gambler again, and then he frowned quizzically. "Say, isn't that a knife sticking outta your coat?"

Ki answered for the gambler, "He was trying to do what your opponent couldn't. With lead. I thought it wise to discourage him."

Livid, Kendrick blurted, "Why, you slant-eyed—!" And then promptly shut up, seeing Ki smile the same pleasant smile as before.

Now Melville laughed. "Serves you right, you sidewinder," he said to Kendrick, and lifting his father by the shoulders, he began carrying him toward the front. Passing the bar, where the customers were thirstily debating the finer details of his fight, Melville glanced back and grinned at Ki, who had hold of the father's ankles. "I guess I owe you my thanks, Mr . . ."

"Ki."

"Just Ki, no 'mister,'" Jessie added, opening the batwings.

Outside, Melville said, "Our wagon's by the barber shop." Starting across the street, he gave Jessica a sidelong appraisal, seeming to want to say something, but only managing to clear his throat a number of times. Finally it came out: "Maybe I shouldn't ask this, Miss Star—uh, Jessie— but are you . . . *with* Ki?"

"You bet. Ki's my guardian and sometime chaperone," she explained teasingly, intrigued by the way Melville's bruised mouth went from a crestfallen droop when he'd asked, to a smiling curve when she'd answered.

Melville stopped in back of a scruffy one-horse farm wagon, whose swaybacked horse dozed placidly at the hitching rail. Opening the wagon's tailgate to climb up inside, Melville started to speak again with faltering embarrassment.

"This is plumb shameful. Please don't think the worse of me or Dad, Jessie. It's mostly on account of him being so powerful lonely and sad, ever since my mother died four years ago."

"I understand, Daryl. Misery makes it easy for men like Halford and Kendrick to take advantage—and take your money."

"You don't know the half of it. We're in hock up to our ears to Kendrick, and we'd have to sell out or simply give him the whole blamed Spraddled M, if we ever had to pay him off all at once."

"You think he's rigged the games to win it?"

"He doesn't want our ranch," Melville replied, as he and Ki slid his father into the wagon bed. "Besides, Dad plays so badly, Kendrick would have to cheat to lose. What makes you ask, Jessie?"

"Nothing I can pinpoint. But the way the man you beat rose to Kendrick's defense makes me wonder a little bit if they haven't got something going between them."

"Nope, that tussle was personal 'tween me and Volpes. We've locked horns before, but nothing like this, and I suppose I shouldn't have lost my temper. But he's been swaggering and bullying around too long, and needed the stuffing knocked outta him." Melville jumped down and untied the horse, adding sheepishly, "Think he knocked some stuffing outta me, too. Anyway, maybe this'll be a lesson for Cap'n Ryker to keep him on a shorter leash."

"Ryker? Guthried Ryker?"

"Yeah. Know him?"

"Strictly by reputation," Jessie said grimly.

"Well, Volpes is Ryker's foreman. He's mean enough

to steal the blanket outta his mother's kennel, but he's kinda at odds with Kendrick and Halford, him working for Cap'n Ryker and all."

"How's that?"

"Well, when Kendrick and Halford arrived here about this time last year, they bought the old saloon and put options on some other properties like the hotel, and generally began acting like bigshots. Then Cap'n Ryker showed up with even more money to spend speculating, and naturally it's stirred up resentments and competition."

Jessie was still perplexed. "That much makes sense. But if Kendrick and Halford are interested in gaining property . . ."

"Sure are," Melville said, nodding, as he climbed up onto the wagon seat. "Them and Cap'n Ryker, squabbling over this and that like two dogs over a bone, to see who'll wind up lording it over the other."

"Then why'd you tell me Kendrick doesn't want your ranch?"

"Because that's what he's told us, Jessie. Says he's only interested in town property, money-making property. Says if he took over, he'd have to abandon it and write it off as a total loss, or else try to run it and end up scratching and starving like we are. He says he'd rather have us make payments to him like a loan, than to have us hand over a spread of skin and bones and worthless dust."

Jessica pursed her lips, pondering for a moment, suspicious of saintly gamblers unwilling to rake in the entire pot the instant it was won. And her brief exposure to Kendrick had not left her impressed with his charitable qualities. She gazed skeptically up at Melville, asking, "Have you offered the ranch to him, Daryl?"

"No, and I don't aim to, unless I'm forced. But speaking of our worthless ranch, I'd best be getting Dad home to bed. Are you still planning to ride out to the Flying W tomorrow morning?"

"At the crack of dawn. Though I wish we could go now, and not waste time spending a night at the hotel," Jessie replied, then turned to Ki. "We are staying there, aren't we?"

Ki nodded. "It's all arranged. Luggage too."

"Well, you just remember that fork in the road," Melville said. "When you pass our place tomorrow, Jessie, you stop in."

"Thanks, we might, if it won't be any trouble."

"No trouble, no trouble a-tall, 'cepting you don't come a-calling like you're expected to. *Then* there'll be trouble." Grinning broadly, Melville released the brake and lashed the reins, and the horse started plodding down the street, the wagon creaking behind it.

Jessica stood beside Ki, watching Melville slowly haul his besotted father home. Daryl was a smooth hairpin, she had to admit; and he already had so many problems that she certainly didn't want to cause him the slightest bit more trouble. So of course she'd visit.

★

Chapter 5

Moving to the boardwalk, Jessica and Ki watched the departing wagon, Ki remarking, "I looked for you at the sheriff's, Jessie. He told me he'd met up with a dratted female of your description, but otherwise he couldn't help any."

"You can say that again, Ki," Jessie replied with disgust. "How'd you know to find me in the saloon?"

"That's where the thick of the uproar was. Where else would you be?" Smiling, Ki took a pocketful of .38 cartridges from his vest and handed them to Jessica, adding: "These are from four boxes I bought. The rest I put in your room."

"Thanks." Loading her revolver, she glanced at the bath house next to the barber shop. "Does the hotel have a bath?"

"Two. Fifty cents extra, fresh water daily, reheated noon and evening, and I've already reserved the one on our floor for us."

"That's a relief," she sighed, starting along the board-walk. She felt grubby and unkempt and in need of a good scrub, from all that had occurred since the ambush. But the bath house, like most cow-town bath houses, would be a male preserve where men would mingle, arguing such weighty issues as women and liquor. She had little interest in bathing with them and airing her differences.

Ki fell in beside Jessie, and they walked in the same direction as the still-visible wagon. He hadn't been blind to her interest in the ruggedly handsome rancher, but neither was he so crass as to pry, other than to ask, "Daryl, did you say his name was?"

"Daryl? Why, yes, Daryl Melville, and his father, Tobias."

"He seems to be shouldering a heavy load."

"I believe he is," Jessie replied, and briefly sketched what she'd learned. "And call it a hunch or feminine intuition, Ki, but I also believe there's some kind of link between what's happening to Daryl and what's happening to Mrs. Waldemar."

"What?"

"I don't know," Jessie said grimly. "Not yet."

They entered the combination telegraph and post office that butted against one side of the hotel. Approaching a wizened oldster who sat behind a barred window, Jessica asked, "Are you acquainted with the owners of the Thundermug Saloon?"

"Yes'm. Halford and Kendrick, know 'em well."

"Know their first names? And where they're from?"

That almost stumped the grizzled clerk, but after scratching his chin thoughtfully, he answered, "Woodrow and Barney, I recollect. Can't say positive where they hail from, 'cepting they've gotten and sent mail and wires to an' from back East, Washington way."

"You're a dear," Jessie said, dimpling a big thank-you smile. She then composed a long telegram that caused the clerk, sworn to secrecy by the rules of the telegraph company, to regard her with even livelier interest. Addressed

45

to the Circle Star ranch in Texas, her message directed that a large draft of money be relayed, and a quick investigation be done on Woodrow Halford and Barney Kendrick, both from Washington, D.C.

"Hold all replies for either me or my friend," Jessica instructed, indicating Ki. "Nobody else, no matter what you're told."

After paying the clerk, they stepped back out onto the street, Ki turning automatically toward the hotel. But Jessica, shaking her head, said, "There're a few things I wish to buy first, now that we're spending the night. Or do you want to meet me here later?"

"No, I haven't anything special to do," Ki replied, and began to walk with Jessica back up toward the general store. "I hired a stablehand at the livery to fetch our things from the cabin, but I doubt he'll return much before nightfall. Oh, and I also rented two saddle horses, a pair of matching bays. The hostler assured me they can be hitched to a buckboard, if you prefer."

"I don't. My suspicion is that before we're through, we'll be having to ride where there aren't any trails."

In the store, Jessie took her time perusing the slim stock of ladies' articles. At length she decided on a plaid flannel shirt to replace her ruined blouses; a calico wrapper and a frilly Empire-style nightgown made of fine nainsook; a bar of castile soap; a box of hairpins; and a traveling set consisting of a Russian bristle hairbrush, nail and toothbrushes, and an imitation ebony comb, all packed in a seal-grain leather case.

Ki, bored silly, made the common male error of asking, "Just what are you planning to do with all that, Jessie?"

"Well, I don't plan to wear filthy clothes after I've bathed, and I don't plan to sleep naked in any hotel," she declared with womanly logic, "and I certainly don't plan to go visiting tomorrow looking dirty and smelling and with my hair all in a tangle."

From the store, they went to the hotel. The Grand Continental may not actually have been grand, but it had a distinct air of faded gentility. Its oak front door had an oval window in it, thick and bevelled, with chintz curtains hanging behind it. There was a well-worn but clean carpet of flowing rose pattern on the lobby floor, and through the scarlet .portiers toward the rear was a dining room with a crystal chandelier and linen settings. The wiry, thin-lipped, gimlet-eyed clerk at the reception desk had a different air about him, that of *eau de lilac,* and was obviously an insufferable prig.

Collecting her key, Jessica asked, "Is there a laundry service?"

"Of course," the clerk said with a sniff. "Anything accepted by eight in the evening will be washed and ironed and delivered by morning."

Jessica took her purchases to her room, which was on the second floor, at the rear. The room was in keeping with the rest of the hotel, with a plain bureau, a drab armchair, and a large wardrobe sporting a full-length, discolored mirror. The bed, though, looked clean and comfortable. On the side of the room opposite the bed, a dreary blue curtain hung from a rail, covering, she assumed, a communicating door to Ki's room.

She opened the window a crack, to let out the mustiness, glancing out at the roof of the sheriff's office, and then down at the dark, narrow alley that ran between it and the side of the hotel. As a view, it left much to be desired. She pulled the blind, and after lighting the kerosene banquet lamp on the bureau, she locked the door after her, and went back down to Ki in the lobby.

They ate an early dinner in the dining room, the food palatable if not interesting, the waiter surly and prone to swatting flies with his serving tray. The young stableboy arrived with their luggage, and after he'd left with a generous tip, Jessie and Ki ordered brandy and coffee, and sat discussing what little they knew.

When it was time for her bath, Jessie returned to her room, where she reloaded her derringer, stripped naked, and put on her new wrapper. She bundled what she'd been

47

wearing with her clothes from the trunk, then took them next door to Ki, asking him to give them to the clerk downstairs.

Then, gathering her toiletries and locking the door behind her, Jessica placed the room key in her wrapper pocket along with her derringer, and went down the corridor to the bathroom. The hook on the bathroom door worked, but just in case, she folded the wrapper so the derringer could be quickly reached from the galvanized tub of tepid water. Cautiously satisfied, she slipped into the tub and settled down in the water for a long, well-deserved soak.

Ki, meanwhile, was deciding that he might as well add some of his own dirty clothes to the bundle Jessie had given him. Tossing in most everything except his jeans, vest, and rope-soled slippers, he waited until he heard Jessica close and safely latch the bathroom door, then left his room and walked down to the lobby.

The twit of a clerk wasn't there. The only person in the otherwise deserted lobby was the girl who cleaned the rooms and made the beds. Ki recalled passing her in the upstairs corridor earlier that day, when he'd first checked in, while she'd been carrying a stack of linens similar to the bundle of clothing he now had in hand. She was now perched on a rickety stool behind the reception desk, concentrating so hard on the game of solitaire she was playing that she failed to notice Ki's approach.

"Excuse me," Ki said.

Stiffening, the girl hastily began to gather the dog-eared cards together, as if he'd caught her doing something very wrong.

"You don't have to stop," Ki said.

"Oh, I should," she replied guiltily. "If Uncle Humphrey catchs me sinning like this, he'll whup me good."

She was a vivid creature, as fiercely pretty as a panther kitten. About twenty, Ki judged, with flaming red hair and great amethyst-blue eyes set in a freckled, tanned face, and with a wide red mouth that was slowly beginning to soften into a relieved smile.

48

"Uncle Humphrey?" Ki asked. "The clerk?"

"And manager, and owner," the girl explained. "He's out for dinner right now, and I'm just holding down the fort till he gets back. That can be a spell at times, but if you want to come back..."

"No, I only want to leave some laundry."

"Well, you can put what you've got 'round back here."

Ki moved to the end of the counter and dumped the bundle. He could now see that the girl was wearing a cheap muslin dress cut rather high on the knees, laundry-boiled over the years almost to the transparency of lace gauze. Her legs were long and bare, her feet encased in low-cut moccasins. He also noticed that although her body was slender and wasp-waisted, she had the large, succulent breasts and thighs of a mature woman built for breeding.

She twisted on the tall stool and regarded the bundle suspiciously. "You've got some lady's things in there, too."

"Miss Starbuck's."

She paused thoughtfully, then said, "Are you two...?"

Ki chuckled. "Not in the way you're thinking."

She giggled and then neither of them said anything more for a while. She just kept looking at Ki, appraising his tight-fitting jeans and vest and his bronzed, muscular form that they barely covered, until her scrutiny and the silence grew embarrassing.

"I hope Uncle Humphrey doesn't come back and find me sitting here doing nothing," the girl said at last. "He doesn't like me to become familiar with the hotel guests, he says. He's afraid something might happen to me, I guess."

Ki grinned. "What kind of something?"

"Oh...you know. Men in here all the time, coming and going. Uncle Humphrey gets powerful mad if I stop and talk to any of them."

"And you never do?"

"I am now, ain't I?"

She lifted her brows when she said that, and looked sideways at Ki. And Ki found himself wondering if there was anything under that dress of hers. Somehow he thought not. There wasn't any reason to believe that it was the only thing she was wearing, but he got the idea, and then he tried imagining what it was like beneath it.

It didn't take much to imagine her breasts. Her lips were full and red; big nipples, then, strawberry in size and color. She had fire-red hair. Between her legs would also be a frothing mass of red, bushy between the cheeks of her big solid rump.

Ki licked his lips. "And is your uncle right about it?"

"What do you think?"

Ki glanced down at the bundle, then across the lobby toward the door, then finally back to the girl. What a vixen, he thought; she exuded sex like her uncle smelled of lilac perfume. He needed her like he needed a bad case of poison ivy, but if a woman's offering, a man will take, even if he has to get off his deathbed for her.

Huskily, he answered, "I think I know what you need."

She sat with a light smirk on her face and then, because she evidently wanted him to make the first move, Ki stepped over the laundry and went to her stool. The girl tilted her face up to him and pressed her lips to his, her tongue darting between his teeth.

Ki held one hand on the stool to keep it from falling over, and slid his other hand over her shoulder, down her dress front. She wriggled some but didn't object, and in a second he was massaging one of her breasts. All things considered, she had damn big breasts for her size, because Ki didn't think she could weigh more than a hundred pounds, but her breasts would have worn well on any woman. She didn't say a word when he started kneading them, but after a long moment she broke her kiss and watched his hand caressing her nipples.

"'I wonder why she ain't trying to fight me,'" she said. "Is that what you're thinking? Why I'm not putting up any struggle?"

"I'm not thinking at all right now."

"All right. But you wonder just the same, I'll bet. I do, I know. And I don't know the answer. I can't imagine why

50

I'm such a pushover. I'm one of those girls who're easy to get, I guess."

"This stool is liable to collapse," Ki said, wanting to change the subject. "Let's either stop or go somewhere."

"I can't leave the desk. We can do it here."

"Your uncle or somebody might come in."

"Maybe. But let's try it anyway and find out." She slipped from his embrace and went to the front door, snapping the catch on the lock and pulling down the window shade. *This is crazy,* Ki thought as she turned and walked back toward him. But her eyes had that vacant, burnt expression that some women got when they were ready to be seduced, and she was breathing hard, as though there weren't enough air in the lobby. Here was blatant challenge, here was passion deluxe. And what man could turn his back on that?

The girl went around the end of the counter and settled down on Ki's bundle of laundry. Slowly, sensuously, she stretched back across the dirty clothing, her dress hiking up above her knees, and she crossed her arms behind her head and gazed invitingly up at him.

Ki sat beside her, and she said, "Don't undress me."

"I'd like to see you naked."

She rubbed her leg against his, and pulled her dress up a little. "I know. It's better when you're naked, but you were right, Uncle Humphrey or somebody could come along."

"Has your uncle ever caught you doing this?"

"Almost. I had to hide in a closet for two hours."

Ki eased her dress higher and saw that she was wearing a pair of short lacy pantaloons, tied by a drawstring at her waist. "Don't wrinkle my dress in back," she said, arching her bottom so he could get it up from under her and spread it out beneath her back. "I guess I'm stupid, letting you do this at all. How'd you know I would? You didn't seem to be worried about me raising hell or anything."

Ki untied the drawstring and began to take her pantaloons off. They were tight from having been washed and shrunk

51

a lot, and were hard to slip over her hips. "I don't know," he replied.

That seemed to satisfy the girl. She helped him tug her pantaloons down past her knees and off her feet.

That big fluff of crimson hair stuck out on her just as he knew it would. He ran his hands across her belly and thighs and dipped down between her legs, stroking her rounded slit. Her legs spread, and she slid lower against the bundle when he hooked his fingers under her pubic hair and speared inside her moist canal.

Still fingering her, Ki used his other hand to unbuckle his jeans and open his fly. She reached, clutching the shaft of this erection and stroking him delicately, as he struggled to lower his pants down around his ankles.

"You stay dressed too," she whispered hoarsely, and wrapped her left arm around his neck, drawing him up and over her, the hand clasping his hardness, guiding it into her warm moisture.

Ki felt himself sinking inside her a long way before he realized how tight she was. He paused then and looked down at her. She was smiling all over. "Don't stop," she said. "It feels good."

He lanced deeper into her again, and this time he could almost feel the juice springing out of her. He began to thrust very hard then, and she seemed to grow even tighter around him, until every time he would pound into her, she would gasp, shuddering, from the squeezing impact. Yet she kept smiling and undulating her buttocks on the pile of dirty laundry, eager for more. There was nothing timid or gentle about this union, Ki thought.

Her hips writhed and pumped under him, her thighs clasping him as if she would hold him in her forever. She began to moan, and her eyes closed, her fingers stroking down over his buttocks as she tried to match Ki's quickening movements. Her moans grew deeper, more prolonged, and she caught at his thighs where they were pressed against the undersides of hers, pulling them at her while her mouth opened and closed as if she were gasping for air.

Then, as her moanings became continuous and high-pitched, the girl began babbling, "Fast, fast, fast, fast..." in a cascade of incoherent emotion. Her hands clutched him savagely, digging into his thighs as her face contorted and her whole body shivered in a series of convulsions.

"Ahhh..." she mewed, as her wet passage compressed around Ki's surging shaft, the force of her orgasm drawing the breath from her lungs in a furious, aching sigh.

As he felt the girl gripping him in her ecstatic release, Ki burrowed deeper, pressing and grinding against her for seconds without pumping his hips. Then he withdrew, thrust slowly in again—and again—and with a final deep thrust, his own climax erupted far up inside her welcoming belly.

Slowly he settled down over her soft warm body, and he lay, crushing her breasts and belly with his weight, until his immediate satiation began to wane. Finally he rolled from her and gently stroked her quivering breasts.

The girl smiled at him with lazy, satisfied eyes. "I guess if Miss Starbuck's and your clothes didn't need washing before," she whispered, "they sure do now..."

While Ki was down romancing the girl, Jessica was relaxing sleepily in her bath. Eventually stirring from her lethargy, she sat up and began to soap her breasts and loins, every inch of her trim yet voluptuous body. Kneeling then, she lathered her long blonde hair, then bent, with the nipples of her distended breasts brushing the water, to rinse off the lather. Briskly she dried herself with a large, fluffy jacquard towel. Her nude flesh tingled, her skin glowing a burnished pink, as she slipped her wrapper on again, collected her toiletries, and left the bathroom.

Padding barefoot along the corridor again, she unlocked her door and found a man in her room. He was stooping over her trunk, one hand on its open lid, the other pawing through her set-up tray. Hearing her enter, he straightened and turned, his clothes grubby work denims and shirt, his face lean-jawed and the color of old paper.

"Well, well, what have we here?" the man said, ogling.

"A burglar, that's what," Jessica retorted sarcastically, in no mood to tolerate the way the man was studying her nudity under the clinging wrapper. She drew out her derringer and pointed it at him. "It's a bit early in the evening for larceny, isn't it?"

"Whoa there, lady, let's not be hasty," the man said, abruptly losing interest in ogling her. "Little mistake in the room, is all. Mayhaps I'm a little drunk too."

"Get out, and I'll call the matter closed, if not forgotten."

"Yes, ma'am, just what I had in mind," he said nervously, sidling out around her and into the hallway. "Let's leave it at that."

The man rushed pell-mell down the corridor. Jessica waited until he'd vanished down the staircase, then examined the door lock and jamb plate, finding they hadn't been forced. She wasn't surprised.

Closing and relatching the door, Jessica figured the incident wasn't worth disturbing Ki about. What could be gained? The man was gone, and had gotten nothing except an eyeful and a scare.

Discarding the wrapper, she slid the flowing nightgown down over her head, and discovered that it was a size smaller than her figure demanded. She smoothed it out as best she could, the fabric like a lover's clasp, squeezing her breasts and pressing around her thighs and buttocks. She continued trying to stretch the gown looser, as she stood in front of the wardrobe mirror, brushing her damp hair and pinning it up so she could sleep on it.

Eventually satisfied, Jessica blew out the oil lamp on the bureau and climbed into bed. She was asleep the instant her head hit the pillow.

She was awakened by Ki.

She felt his presence at first and, opening her eyes, saw him moving through the connecting doorway into her darkened room, wearing only his jeans, his bare feet noiseless on the floor. When she sat up, still foggy with sleep, he put a finger to his lips as a signal for absolute silence, and pointed at the window with his other hand.

Jessica froze, breathless. For an agonizing moment she

heard nothing, and she realized it was probably sometime between three and five in the morning, in that predawn stillness when most everybody is sleeping their soundest, and those awake are at their most relaxed. And when Ki was at his most alert.

Then, from below the window, against the side of the building, came a slight scraping noise and a soft squeak of stressed wood. Ki was beside the window now, poised motionless, staring intently at the drawn blind like a cat watching a mousehole. Gently, Jessica rose, slipping from the covers and easing over to the other side of the window. Ki gestured for her to back away, but before she could, the sash creaked slowly higher and the blind began to quiver.

A hand raised the bottom edge of the blind. Whoever was out there then stuck his other hand underneath, gripping two dynamite sticks tied together, fuses sparking and hissing.

Ki pounced. He grabbed hold of those two hands by their wrists and thrust them back out the window, leaning way out before letting go with a final shove. The dynamite went with them, and so did the blind, ripping off its roller to flap out like a flying tail.

A startled howl, which had begun at the height of the window, was swiftly falling away and down. Jessica, peering out the window with Ki, saw a tall spindly ladder teetering in an arc away from the hotel wall, its legs firmly rooted in the alley below. The hunching silhouette of a man was perched on its top rungs, clinging helplessly as he was catapulted backwards toward the sheriff's stone office.

The ladder struck the edge of the building, toward the rear of the structure where the jail cells would be. The man was flung onto the roof, his howl cut off as the dynamite detonated with a terrific, brilliant flash. The hotel quivered, glass shattering, while down across the alley, the rear quarter of the sheriff's office hurtled out, stone, beams, and masonry cycloning up and about in a blinding white cloud. The roof collapsed in the hole the explosion had punched, fire blossoming through the wreckage.

By the suddenly sprouting incandescence, Jessica saw

Deputy Oakes stumble out the front door, wearing long red underwear and nothing else. Other doors and windows were opening, the street swirling in a confusion of shouting men and women both dashing about, cursing and questioning, gaping at the ruined building that was now being consumed by hungry flames.

Ki turned, surveying Jessica. "Are you all right?"

She nodded, though she was still shaky, still dazzled by the glare, her head whirling from the concussion of the blast. "Somebody doesn't like us," she said, smiling weakly. "I can't imagine who."

"And he knew where to find us. If I hadn't been lucky enough to hear that ladder brushing up against the wall, he would've succeeded," Ki added, slamming the window and starting back to the connecting door. He paused before closing it to say reassuringly, "But I think that's all he'll try for tonight. Sweet dreams."

Jessica went back to bed and pulled the covers up close around her neck. She listened to the continuing noise from the street, and watched the reflection of the fire in the wavy glass pane of her window, and she wondered what tomorrow would bring in the way of death.

She lay there a long time before going to sleep again.

Chapter 6

The rising sun had scarcely cleared the mountains behind them when Jessica and Ki turned at the fork in the road west of Eucher Butte. They rode for the next two hours through a vast upland basin that was hemmed in by the river to the south, and by granite-toothed and canyon-gashed foothills ahead and to the north, the peaks of the Laramie Range towering beyond, seeming to float above the horizon on a sea of morning mist.

The trail kept to a course that meandered toward the foothills, the broad sweep of the basin slowly falling behind, being replaced by increasingly rugged country of tumbling creeks and high, timbered plateaus. The sun had become hot and bright against their backs by the time the two riders reined in their mounts before a narrow lane that cut away from the trail. A board nailed to a tree beside the lane bore the brand of the Spraddled M.

Heeling their bays into a trot, they followed the rutted lane through a belt of spruce and yellow pine, then down into a verdant swale speckled with the first buds of spring. Along a stream that flowed across one side of the swale were strung the few low buildings of a ranch: a long, thin, cabinlike ranch house; a squarer bunkhouse, against which leaned a grub shack; a clapboard barn and a scattering of sheds; and a pole corral in which a few horses stood.

The Melville spread did not look rich, Jessica thought as they approached the stretch of bare yard in front of the ranch house. But it was neat, and the buildings appeared to be in good repair, showing a desire to work hard and do the best with what there was.

A gallery ran the length of the ranch house. There was a small amount of clutter and discarded saddlery at each end of it, but in the middle, next to the front door, was a rocking chair. Sitting in the rocker was Tobias Melville, clad in a loose-hanging vest and denims of the range, and a plaid shirt not unlike the one Jessica was wearing. A faded bandanna was knotted around his throat, a thatch of white hair peeking from beneath a floppy-brimmed, sweat-stained hat.

Daryl Melville was standing nearby, one boot on the gallery and the other on the ground, as if he couldn't make up his mind whether to come or to go. He had on a clean set of clothes, and was hatless, his hair slicked and combed. But he was also wearing, Jessica saw, the same dark scowl as he'd worn yesterday, when he'd been angered at Deputy Oakes, and then later in the saloon.

Daryl and his father were looking at whoever was in the buggy parked alongside the gallery by the rocker. The buggy had a piano-box body and a leather quarter-top, and was hitched to a sleek dapple gray. Because the fancy top blocked their view, neither Jessica nor Ki could tell who was in it until they rode all the way up to the gallery. But they could hear a deep, well-modulated voice coming from within, saying to the Melvilles:

"Let's be realistic. You don't have anything to sell but

debts and scarecrow cattle, but I'll take them to secure your range—"

"Hello, there," Daryl interrupted, smiling as he spotted Jessica and Ki drawing near. "Sure glad you could make it."

And the words from the buggy came to an abrupt halt.

Two men were sitting in the buggy, their eyes veiled, as Jessica and Ki pulled up to the gallery. The one holding the reins was a bucktoothed, hatchet-faced man with an impassive, secretive expression. The other was middle aged, sporting bristly muttonchops, his once handsome face and deep-socketed eyes webbed with lines of dissipation. And it was obvious from his apparel that he was more accustomed to rich city reveling than hardscrabble ranch life, wearing as he was a pair of flat-heeled patent-leather shoes, a square-crowned Governor hat, and a dark brown town suit of expensive broadcloth, its jacket unbuttoned to relieve his paunch.

The tense silence stretched on, until Tobias Melville rocked back and remarked affably, "Sure got peaceful of a sudden."

"Yes, well, where're my manners?" Daryl said hastily, clearing his throat. "Dad, I'd like you to meet Miss Jessie Starbuck."

"Heard something about you this morning," the father said, grinning. His gaunt face was creased with wrinkles, but his eyes, as black as his son's, were sharp and bright as he looked Jessica over. He seemed to like what he saw. "Call me Toby, Jessie."

"And her friend, Ki," Daryl continued.

"Heard about you too, feller. But you ain't Mexican."

"Mexican?" Ki echoed, nonplussed.

"Ain't Mexicans the ones who're best with knives?"

"Pa!" Daryl snapped, scowling afresh. But Toby just continued grinning unregenerately, looking incredibly chipper after his long bout of drinking. Jessica, smothering a laugh, thought it was amazing, the vitality these leathery old ranchers seemed to have.

Forging ahead, Daryl said, "Cap'n Ryker? Let me intro—"

"We're aquainted," Ryker cut in, a sharp edge to his mellow voice. "That is, we know each other by reputation. As president of Acme Packers, I am well aware of my competitors, of which Starbuck is definitely one. As I'm sure Starbuck is similarly aware of me."

"Oh, you bet we are," Jessica said.

"The Captain's trying to buy us out," Toby explained, obviously tickled by his chance to stir things up. "Plans to run us together with the Flying W, when he takes that place over, too."

"Now, now, Mr. Melville, I said no such thing to you."

"But that's what you've got in mind, ain't it, Cap'n?"

"Well, I suppose I'm forced to admit it is," Ryker replied gravely, and turned from Toby to Jessica. "To be perfectly honest, Miss Starbuck, my company needs the same thing yours does—a constant, reliable supply of beef without the fluctuating prices and conditions we've all experienced. I'm here on behalf of Acme, trying to persuade the smaller ranchers to sell out to one large combine, rather than join a cooperative of the sort you've been attempting to establish. I'm afraid that if I succeed, the ranches involved would no longer be able to honor their commitments with Starbuck."

Jessica clucked her tongue and looked downcast. "You understand if I hope your plans fail. But will you be staying permanently?"

"Goodness, no. When my negotiations are finished, win or lose, I'll leave whatever I've obtained in capable hands, and move on."

"Then you might as well move on from here, Cap'n Ryker," Daryl said sternly. "Unless you're willing to meet our price."

"Thirty thousand?" Ryker's chuckle was amiable. "My good man, I could buy all of Eucher Butte for that much money."

"Be my guest. Halford and Kendrick mightn't agree, though."

"Ah, yes, Kendrick. Now listen, I'm offering a fair price, more than a fair price, almost double what you owe Kendrick—what, in effect, you'd be getting for your ranch by turning it over to him."

"Don't intend to settle for Kendrick's price, either. We intend to keep it for all it's worth. Thirty thousand worth."

"You may not have that choice much longer," Ryker continued in his shrewd, persuasive voice. "Oh, I understand how you feel, how you believe your ranch is worth a great deal, how you place a high value on the sweat and tears you've spent improving it. But consider this—will your crew shed more blood to help you keep it?"

Daryl stepped forward, fists clenched. "Is that a threat?"

"Simple advice. Even supposing Kendrick held off claiming your ranch as payment, there's a ruinous crime wave going on in this area that Deputy Oakes seems incapable of stopping. If it continues as it has, it could ultimately rob you of all your assets, and leave you crippled, in a worse position to bargain than you're in now."

"Our land'll remain. Like you said, that's all you want."

Ryker threw up his hands in frustration. "You're not being sensible, son. Very well, I won't pursue this further this morning. But I'll be at my Block-Two-Dot in case you want to get off your high horse and talk down on the ground. Good day to you all."

With a tip of his hat and a nudge at his driver, Ryker sat back in the seat, looking sourly exasperated. Behind the dapple gray, the buggy veered about and jounced, swaying, out of the yard.

Apart from the noise of the departing buggy, and the clucking of some scrawny hens foraging by a pile of manure, nothing stirred for a long moment. Then Jessica, referring to Roby's initial comment, said lightly, "Yes, it certainly is pleasant and peaceful here."

"Like blazes it's peaceful," Toby snorted. "We and the boys are shot at, our cows are run off . . . not that I'd allow Cap'n Snake-eyes the satisfaction of hearing tell."

"Snake-eyes?"

"That's what Dad calls Ryker's Block-Two-Dot brand."

"Looks just like dice showing twos," Toby added, grinning.

Jessica laughed. "But aren't you trying to sell to him?"

Daryl shook his head. "We were only funning him, Jessie. We picked the figure of thirty thousand 'cause nobody'd be dumb enough to pay such a price. C'mon, step down and rest a spell."

"Thanks, but we're awfully late as it is."

"I know a shortcut," Daryl offered hopefully, and when Jessica didn't refuse, he grinned, saying, "Wait a minute, I'll saddle up."

As Daryl began sprinting for the corral, Toby yelled, "You ain't leaving me ahind to rot, blast you!" He lurched up out of his rocker and chased bandy-legged after his son. "Hell, you get lost goin' to the outhouse! You better let me do the pointin'!"

A short while later, the four were riding as a group across Spraddled M range, Daryl on a linebacked buckskin gelding, and his father on a tubby roan mare. They headed west-northwest over mountain meadows and among thick stands of spruce, fir, and lodgepole pine, at one point spotting Spraddled M hands chousing a small bunch of young stuff down by some creek brakes. Then Daryl shifted to a slightly more northern track, and climbed higher along a tangent through the forested benches and rocky slopes.

Eventually, their hard-breathing horses struggling with the steepened grade, they topped a ridge and Daryl reined in. Ahead stretched the vista of a wide, shallow valley, through which coursed the wavering thread of a stream. Beyond the stream was the distant outline of a ranch, its cluster of buildings vaguely resembling the Spraddled M's, a windmill in its yard briskly revolving, sunlight glinting faintly off the whirring blades.

"Like the view?" Daryl asked cheerfully.

Jessica nodded. "It's beautiful out here."

"Well, it looks better'n usual. We had a good snowpack this winter, and spring's been pretty wet so far, but generally we suffer from poor runoffs and low rainfall. A couple of years it's gotten as bad as being drought-dry." He jiggered his buckskin closer to Jessica's bay, until they were almost touching stirrups. "That's the Flying W you see down there. Actually, it was doing fine, despite the weather and all, till Waldemar met with his accident."

"And now?"

"It's going to hell in a handbasket. Frankly, I'm glad Dad is coming along. He and Uriah—Mr. Waldemar— loved feuding over cribbage a lot, and I think he misses him almost as much as he does my mother. But, 'cept for the funeral, Dad hasn't been by to pay respects to Mrs. Waldemar, and I know she must be feeling lonesome and miserable about everything, and could do with an old friend cheering her up some."

"You leave me to my own socializin', son," Toby snapped.

Daryl turned to his father, grinning. "You an' Uriah, the orn'riest pair of mules ever born, I swear." He kneed his horse forward, and with Jessica following closely, Ki and Toby trailing a few feet behind, they began their slow, winding descent into the valley.

Jessica said to Daryl, "That accident was pretty convenient. I understand Mr. Waldemar refused to sell out to Ryker."

"I don't know what you mean by his death being convenient, Jessie, but yeah, Uriah wanted nothing to do with Cap'n Ryker. There was bad feeling 'tween them right from the start, when the Cap'n first moved onto the Block-Two-Dot. It's way over in the next valley, and it's probably the largest and richest of the smaller spreads. Anyway, Uriah was a tough, stubborn, but honest cowman, and you know how some of them can feel about Easterners taking over spreads."

"The ol' grunt-and-grab," Toby added from behind.

Daryl twisted in his saddle again. "Dad, you're only saying that 'cause that's what Uriah used to say. But if you consider it from Ryker's angle, he's buying up a wad of mortgages and debts, offering a way out, often the only way out, from bankruptcy."

"Maybe," Jessica said, "but he drives a hard bargain."

"Why shouldn't he? He's a businessman. We're the damn fools who've bitten off more'n we can chew, trying to make a go with a handful of cattle and a wagonload of furniture. He's not accountable if we end up dragging ourselves down into poverty and misery."

"He is if he helps do the dragging."

"He doesn't have to, Jessie. Failure seems to come natural to some folks, just like it's human nature to blame the winner who comes to buy up what's left. A body resents it, resents what's given."

"Maybe Ryker should grow whiskers and drive reindeer," Jessica retorted, angered to hear Ryker described as a benefactor for gobbling up other peoples' property and dreams. On the other hand, Daryl was speaking without having her information, her black book, her background and experience in dealing with such skunks. And at this point she didn't feel ready to educate him, either.

They dropped out of the hills and onto the gently rolling floor of the valley, and for a while rode roughly parallel to the creek. Where the creek was bridged by a wagon road, they turned and followed the road until they reached the home pastures of the Flying W. The windmill appeared first, flickering in the sunlight atop the wrinkled steppes of a hillock. Then, as the road curved around the base of the hillock, the ranch itself came into view, sprawling in the mottled shade of a grove of cottonwoods.

Riding into the yard, Jessica saw a couple of punchers moving around the outbuildings. When they saw who she was, they sped up, and Jessica, smiling inwardly, thought the crew must all be madder than a boil at her. Then, pulling up in front of the ranch house, she eyed its weathered clapboards, dirty and paint-peeling, though its windows were washed and were framed by spotless curtains.

They were dismounting as a graying woman came to the door. She appeared colorless and subdued, with a lurking sadness to her eyes, but she wore a clean house dress, and her hair was neatly plaited and pinned around her head.

"Howdy, Am'belle," Toby greeted, lifting his hat.

"How do, Toby, Daryl." Her voice was throaty and warm. "And you must be Miss Starbuck. Please, all of you, come on in."

At the door, Jessica asked her, "Your crew told you?"

"Did they ever!" Mrs. Waldemar's lips perked with a wry smile. "They larruped in like a posse was after 'em, and got to working bright and early, fit to beat the band. All save Lloyd. He quit."

Jessica frowned, recalling the aggressive Lloyd Nealon. "I'm sorry. That leaves you short a foreman, and that's not what I had in mind. I guess I overstepped my bounds, and I do apologize."

"'Tain't accepted, Miss Starbuck. You did what Uriah would've done, and what I should've done if I'd had the gumption of a ninny." She shut the door and headed for the kitchen, adding, "Now sit. I've got coffee on the stove, and an apple pandowdy in the oven."

Inside, the parlor was meagerly yet tastefully furnished. Jessica and Daryl settle on a horsehair tête-à-tête sofa, while Toby relaxed in an easy chair with his hat balanced on his knees, and Ki stood beside a French marquetry-work side table.

"Don't you want to sit comfortable?" Mrs. Waldemar asked Ki, when she returned from the kitchen bearing a loaded tray.

"No, thank you. I feel quite comfortable standing."

"Ain't used to a saddle, I betcha, and's just sore from our ride," Toby declared. Which was anything but the truth; Ki simply preferred to stand, finding most American stuffed furniture, including beds, too soft and spongy for his taste. But then, Toby probably didn't believe what he was saying anyway, and promptly forgot about it as he started eating the fresh-baked apple pandowdy. "This is plumb scrumptious, Am'belle. Best I've ever tasted."

"If you didn't make yourself so scarce, Toby, you'd find

I can cook more'n that," Mrs. Waldemar replied, as she finished pouring coffee and serving wedges of apple pandowdy. "And you'd also find I'd whup you at cribbage worse'n Uriah ever could." Setting the tray aside, she sat down in an armless reception chair and regarded Jessica appreciatively. "You received my letter. I truly didn't expect anyone to come here about it, but I am most grateful."

"You still suspect your husband was murdered?"

"I've learned nothing to change my mind, Miss Starbuck. I can't say I don't wish to have his killer brought to justice, but I doubt the crime will ever be solved, and nothing can bring Uriah back. No, I must put that behind me, and think of the ranch."

"Well, that's why we're here, Mrs. Waldemar. If you'll allow me, I'd like to take a look at your books and some of your land, and see if we can't come up with a few suggestions to help you."

"Feel perfectly free, and my prayers are with you. The banker and my foreman—that is, my *ex*-foreman—and others who should know have all insisted it's too late, and there's nothing left but to sell."

"Yes, to Ryker. Has he made you a reasonable offer?"

"I can't judge, and I'm not sure it'd matter if I could. It's the only offer; no other buyer is willing to buck the Captain."

"You're bucking him, Am'belle, and good for you."

"You know why I am, Toby. Because Uriah would spin in his grave if I let Captain Ryker buy the Flying W. Besides, the ranch was profitable before, and I can't help believing it can be made so again, if . . ." Mrs. Waldemar paused, getting to her feet and pacing the room, looking troubled and embarrassed as she halted in front of Jessica. "If, Miss Starbuck, you'll bring in some men. Some real men, who won't scat to the tall timber whenever the rustlers cut our herd or torch our graze. Men who won't hesitate to kill."

Jessica studied the coffee in her cup. She finally answered, "Hiring gunhands isn't a solution. It'd only mean we'd have two packs of wolves to get rid of, instead of one."

Mrs. Waldemar sat down heavily. "Of course. Two wrongs never made a right. I'm ashamed of myself for even thinking such a thing."

After a few more minutes of small talk, Mrs. Waldemar ushered Jessica into her late husband's study, and showed her where the books were kept. Spreading the books and related papers out on the study's battered rolltop desk, Jessica began a cursory investigation of the ranch's financial status, and almost immediately found it to be deeply in the red, bordering on collapse.

Beef receipts from the last co-op gather had been spent before Starbuck had paid off, the Flying W's income going to back wages, supply and feed credit chits, and an overdue mortgage payment. Current expenses were not being met, other than a few of the worst bills, which apparently had been paid through withdrawals from Mrs. Waldemar's savings account back in Boston. Rustlers had whittled at the Flying W stock until the latest tally recorded by Nealon revealed less than two hundred three-year-olds, yearlings, and heifers. Even if Starbuck accepted them at top market quotations, Jessica realized that it would barely pay the crew what they were owed.

Squaring her shoulders, Jessica replaced the books and rolled down the top of the old desk. She returned to the parlor, where Ki and Daryl were standing by the sofa, watching Toby and Mrs. Waldemar play cribbage, the scoreboard and cards on the cushion between them.

"I know, it's as bad as I've been told," Mrs. Waldemar sighed dejectedly, glancing up. "The Flying W is finished, beyond recovery, and I should resign myself to losing it to Captain Ryker."

"I'll admit it can't continue as it is," Jessica replied. "But we're here to try to save it, not bury it, and before anything's decided, I want to take a quick tour of the property with Ki."

Daryl grinned. "Well, I'm your guide. Dad?"

Toby shook his head, fuming. "Go ahead, son. Am'belle's just skunked me with pairs royal, but she ain't going to get away with it."

Leaving the ranch house, Jessica, Ki, and Daryl spent the rest of the day in their saddles. The unfenced range of the Flying W took in the valley and some of the broken hills that surrounded it, much of the land having a short, tough grass cover that was not the best, but was adequate for grazing. The hands they encountered appeared to know more or less what they were doing, though the lack of supervision was evident in their choice of tasks. The spread would never be a gold mine, Jessica concluded, but it had once been healthy—and with a lot of luck, leadership, and hard labor, it could be again.

Their inspection took longer than expected, and dusk had fallen by the time they returned to the ranch yard. Dismounting, Daryl asked, "Well, shall we go report to Mrs. Waldemar?"

Jessica, glancing at the lighted windows of the cookshack, said, "Not yet. There's one more thing I want to get straight."

She led the way to the cookshack, noting, as they went, the littered, unkempt appearance of the barn, sheds, and bunkhouse. It shocked and angered her to think how, in just the few short months since Uriah Waldemar's death, the Flying W had declined through indifference and neglect. Amabelle Waldemar was a fine, decent lady who had no experience in running a ranch and, not knowing any better, had placed her trust in the wrong men. If Jessica did no more than turn the ranch around and keep Ryker from grabbing it, it would be adequate reason for having come to Eucher Butte.

Inside the smoky cookshack, the Flying W crew lined both sides of a long plank table, demolishing platters of meat and potatoes, and steaming pots of coffee. At the head of the table was the empty chair of the foreman; Jessica sat down in it and reached for the coffee, while Ki and Daryl stood flanking the door.

The crewmen studiously ignored their presence, other than to dart surly glances in their direction while they ate. Finishing their meal, the men shoved their plates aside and rose to leave.

"Sit tight," Jessica snapped. "You're not through yet."

The crew hesitated, giving her hard, belligerent looks, then slowly settled back on the benches. In the tense hush that followed, Jessica sipped her coffee and thought how they all must be silently wishing she'd go away, preferably straight to hell. Well, she wasn't about to go; she was going to stay and find out how many of *them* were going to go.

Draining her cup, she returned their harsh glares and said, "But in another sense, you're through. Through for good."

One of the feistier hands protested, "Lady, it's not—"

"Miss Starbuck, if you please. And yes, it is."

"Miz Starbuck, okay, but it's not right to fire us now. We came back and worked all day, like you wanted. It's not fair."

"I don't have to fire you. You're firing yourselves, with all your hurrawing on the ranch's time and money. And the rustlers are firing you too, by raiding and looting till the Flying W is stone broke, and Ryker can take it over as a favor." She leaned forward, sternly eyeing the shaken crew. "Ryker says he's planning to form a combine out of the ranches he buys, and you know what that'll mean? It'll mean most of you'll be canned, and those who aren't will have to work twice as hard for half the wages."

Another puncher shrugged. "Nothing we can do to change it."

"That's where you're wrong, dead wrong. You're going to start tomorrow dawn, by weeding out the stock of everything four years and older, and shipping them to Starbuck. We need them like the plague, but it'll help pay your wages, help keep you *hired*. And I want a couple of you to take

69

some Giant powder to the west end of the valley, where the stream flows down out of that long canyon. I found plenty of tracks heading up it, and the cows didn't get there by straying."

The second puncher nodded, brightening. "Not a bad idea. A little blasting up in the rocks oughta close that gap to rustlers."

"It'll also dam the stream," Jessica continued. "It'll form a reservoir to provide extra water for the herd, and for crop irrigation."

That startled a third hand. "Crops? We're not sod-busters."

Jessica favored him with a flinty smile. "It's not hard to learn. And you'd better, because that whole section by the canyon will be fenced off for native hay and maybe some sugar beets. What you don't use for the ranch will be sold as another source of income."

By now the entire Flying W crew was gaping at her. Daryl, as well, was studying her in wonderment. She was moving fast and decisively, this Jessica Starbuck. She was ramrodding hard—which, though unsettling, was also generating fresh enthusiasm.

And then she dropped the bomb. "You're going to need a foreman, what with Nealon gone—and from what I've seen so far, good riddance—so I'm going to ask Toby Melville to stay on awhile, as guest of Mrs. Waldemar. From now on, you'll take your orders from him."

There was an outburst of voices, including Daryl's: "But Jessi—"

She shushed them with a wave of her hand. "Listen, Toby Melville's forgotten more about ranching than most of us will ever learn. And you all get along with the Spraddled M crew, don't you?" When she wasn't contradicted, she forged on: "The two spreads will remain separate. I'm only talking about banding together till we've licked the rustling. A common herd can be defended by fewer men, freeing others for nighthawking—and fighting."

A fifth hand balked at this. "Fighting, like in shooting?

Not me. I was hired to nurse cows, not toss lead."

Jessica nailed him with steel-cold eyes. "You're hired to side the Flying W, a fact you've managed to ignore." Surveying the others, she added, "You're bogged down and sinking fast, and if you hope to save your ranch and your jobs, you're going to have to lay your brains and guts and, by God, all your loyalty on the line."

"By damn, I've heard all the manure I plan to," a puncher way in the back sneered, "and the only reason I say 'manure' is on account of a female's present. Leastwise, she *looks* like a female."

Daryl stiffened. "Hold on, watch your tongue there."

The third Flying W hand who'd spoken now chimed in, "Yeah, Wylie, ain't no call to—"

"Shut up, Croft," the man called Wylie snarled. "Maybe your spine is made outta smoke, but as for me, I've had my fill of bein' lectured at by strange wimmen." He got up from the table, a dark, squat man with a barrel chest and black, beady eyes. "I'm doin' nothin' till Miz Waldemar tosses these troublemakin' talkers offen the ranch. If anybody else feels the same, come with me."

The two burly punchers who'd been flanking him on the bench rose and fell in, swaggering behind Wylie as he began shouldering his way toward the door. Apparently his close buddies, they laughed when he glared at Jessica and taunted, "Yeah, if I craved preacherin', lady, I'd go to Sunday school." Then, turning to Daryl and Ki, he added, growling, "Step aside, 'lessen you wish to get busted apart."

Almost to the front of the table now, he drew abreast of Croft. Foolishly, Croft shifted on the bench and reached out to place a cautioning hand lightly on Wylie's arm. "Simmer down, Wylie," he said. "Hear them out. Maybe these folks've got something to—"

"Leggo!" Wylie wrenched away from Croft's hand as though it were a snake biting his arm, then pivoted and shoved his palm flat into Croft's face. "I'll learn you to shut up!" he snarled, and mashed Croft's head down into his dinner plate with a dull, meaty crunch. Dazed and half-blinded, Croft reeled to one side and began falling off the bench, and Wylie drew back his right foot to kick his boot into Croft's unprotected belly. "I'll learn you good!"

Ki reacted before the kick could land. With an odd smile that masked his anger, he launched himself at Wylie, who immediately turned to meet him with clenched fists. Ki ducked Wylie's first and last punch, catching the puncher's outflung arm and angling to drop to one knee, swinging him into *seoi otoshi,* the kneeling shoulder-throw.

Wylie arched through the air, over the heads of the seated men, and came down on the table, atop the meat platter and the bowl of mashed potatoes. He sprawled there, dazed and breathless.

Even before Wylie hit, Ki was swinging around in the cramped space between the bench and the wall, to check whatever Wylie's two friends might be up to. The nearer one was charging him with outstretched arms, as if he were tackling a drunk in a barroom brawl. Ki chopped the edge of his hand down at the fellow's nose. He purposely held back a little so he would not break it, but it struck forcefully enough to hurt like hell, and tears of pain sprang into the man's eyes. Ki followed through by kicking the man in the side of his knee, collapsing him to one side. He caught his right arm, crunched down on it with his elbow, and then brought his own knee into his hip.

The man dropped to the floor, leaving the way clear for Wylie's second pal to lash out at Ki with his wide leather belt. Ki had already seen this second one slide off his belt and fold it double, which was one of the reasons he'd had to dump the first man, for now he was able to step over the first man and catch hold of the second one's right arm and left shoulder with his hands. At the same time, Ki moved his right foot slightly in back of the man so that as the fellow began tumbling sideways, Ki was able to dip to his right knee and yank viciously. His *hizi otoshi,* or elbow-drop, worked perfectly; the second man catapulted upside-down and collapsed jarringly on top of the first man, flattening them both to the floor.

And Wylie, face purpling with rage, launched himself off the table, a well-honed bowie knife clutched in his right hand. "I'm gonna carve you apart!" he bellowed, slashing at Ki.

Ki calmly stepped aside and then kicked up with his callused foot. His heel caught Wylie smack on his chin, so hard that Wylie flew backwards onto the table again. This time he sprawled cold on his back, staring sightlessly up at the rafters and cobwebbed ceiling of the cookshack.

The rest of the Flying W crew gaped at Wylie, his two moaning pals, and then at Ki with stunned disbelief. They said nothing.

Jessica broke the silence. "If these three want to quit, then they can quit. If any of you others want to quit, you can. Or you can stay. It's up to you, but make up your minds. As I said last night, I don't have the time—and the Flying W doesn't have the time—for you to sit on your butts. Either start kicking or packing."

The feisty hand who'd first spoken, now spoke up again. "Well, boys, I reckon Miz Starbuck might have something. She sure has a powerful persuader, and she's got me convinced. We gotta pitch in and stop the raidin', else we'll all be grub-lining. 'Sides, none of us is safe from a bushwhack bullet 'lessen we do rare up and fight back."

"Okay, count me in."

"We gotta do something, I see that now."

"Sure, we couldn't face Miz Waldemar if we didn't."

A consensus of agreement quickly swelled from the crew, including the one who'd refused to fight. "Might as well," he growled, moodily building a smoke. "Guess it don't make no difference how I bleed, fast or slow. I'll be dead here anyways."

Diplomatically thanking the men for their splendid cooperation, Jessica rose and left the cookshack. Ki followed, amused as ever by how much she was her father's child, equally as competent as Alex Starbuck had been in defusing and mastering tricky negotiations.

Daryl stood momentarily by the shack's open door, staring in bewildered at the sudden and complete change in the crewmen. Then he turned and swiftly caught up with Jessica and Ki, as they were walking toward the ranch house. "Jessie, that was great, but . . ." He faltered, still stunned by her volunteering of his father. "But Dad can't do it, you know how he drinks. He won't want to."

"We've got to make him want to," Jessica replied, and with a twinkle in her eye, she added, "I suspect that between handling those men, and Amabelle Waldemar's cooking and cribbage, Toby's going to find staying here to be a sobering experience."

Toby, when confronted, ranted and blustered. But he didn't argue all that hard, and eventually he caved in with surprising grace. Or maybe it wasn't so surprising.

★

Chapter 7

After enjoying a dinner with all the trimmings, Jessica, Ki, and Daryl bade goodbye to Mrs. Waldemar, who was now feeling greatly heartened, and to Toby, who was crankily washing the dishes, his penalty for having been thoroughly trounced at cribbage. The trio stepped to the barn and re-saddled their fed and rested horses, then rode slowly out of the yard toward the main trail.

Moving alongside Jessica, Daryl said, "I sure do like your notion of combining the two spreads. I think my boys will go for it, once we've pointed out the advantages."

"Problem is, Daryl, it'll only work temporarily. We've stirred up the crew here and stiffened their spines, and maybe we can do the same for yours. But after a while, it's bound to wear off."

"Meanwhile," Ki added, "the rustlers can lie low, waiting

for your crews to grow lax and drift apart before striking again."

"I don't think they'll wait," Daryl responded. "They seem to be a nervy bunch of polecats, and I wouldn't put it past them to try anyway, just to prove they're stronger. Even if they did hold off our spreads a while, they'd still be able to hit the other ranchers."

Jessica nodded. "You're right, there's a good chance of that. But if the other ranchers haven't gotten together before this to protect themselves, there isn't much we can do now to help them."

"Well, there is one thing you can do now," Daryl said with a grin. "You can both come to the Spraddled M and stay overnight. There's lots of room, especially with Dad gone. And Jessica, after watching you twist the Flying W crew around your finger, I'd sure like you around in the morning, when I have my confab with the boys."

"Nice of you to offer, Daryl. Maybe we will, later."

"But I insist. You can't mean to ride half the night, all that long way back to Eucher Butte."

"I don't."

"Then where . . . ?"

"I mean to ride to the Snake-Eyes."

"The Block-Two-Dot?" Startled, Daryl jerked erect in his saddle. "Jessie, by the time you get there, Cap'n Ryker'll probably be in bed, in no mood to welcome a visit."

"I don't want his welcome. I don't want him to know."

"You're talking in riddles, Jessie," he said impatiently.

She reached across and placed her hand fondly on his arm. "I'm sorry. You're simple going to have to take my word for it—for a lot of things, right now."

Daryl gnawed his lower lip, frowning. "All right," he said at last, "I know it's useless to try changing your mind, once it's made up. And I'll take it on faith that you've got good reason. So I'm coming along and making sure you keep outta harm."

"Believe me, Daryl, Ki's very good at that."

Daryl twisted in his saddle to look over at Ki. "I've got

every respect for your fighting abilities, Ki, but you and her don't know the country like I know it." He turned back to face Jessica. "Whatever you're planning to do at Ryker's, it plainly involves sneaking in. Well, I'm the one who can get you there unseen, and if trouble pops, I'm the one who can get you two out."

"We accept," Ki said, before Jessica could answer. "But you'll have to promise to do what we say, when we say it."

"I promise to consider it. Now follow me."

Spurring his buckskin, Daryl led Jessica and Ki northeast across the Flying W valley. When they reached the hills that separated the Flying W from the Block-Two-Dot, they climbed in a wide circle to hit Ryker's spread from almost due north. It took them over an hour to work their way through the jagged, forested heights and down around to where they could first glimpse the ranch.

Spied at a distance, the barns and corrals and other buildings appeared dwarfed by the tall, sheer cliffs surrounding them on three sides. It was as if the Block-Two-Dot were set in a canyon-locked lagoon, facing a gentle sea of waving grass, and fronting a thin beach of roadway that cut in from a nearby pass. And it looked silent and deserted from where they paused, seeming to sleep in the clouded moonlight. But as they watched, a tiny figure left the bunkhouse and strolled to the corral. In a few moments it returned to the bunkhouse, and the yard was empty again.

"They're still awake," Daryl commented dryly.

"Then we'll wait," Ki responded, his eyes surveying the stone walls around the ranch. "Up there." He pointed toward a fault in one cliff face, which formed a steep but not impossible slope to the top.

Skirting the open valley meadow and keeping to the cover of rocks and trees, they eased along the base of the hills until they reached the cliff. Horses and riders struggled up the slope, hooves slipping and gouging out small avalanches of stone and dirt. When they struck the rim, they rested their mounts awhile, then cautiously rode toward a concealed ledge closer above the ranch.

Finally they dismounted and picketed the horses, moving ahead on foot to a flat rock projecting out from the face of the cliff. They slid out and crouched at the edge, pleased to find they could view the dark, corrugated uplands and the bleak mountains beyond; the purple valley pastures that were mottled with the duskier splotches of cattle; the lofty walls of the box canyon in whose notch the shadowed ranch was nestled. Their perch was ideal, and they settled themselves for a long vigil.

Time passed. A few hands left the bunkhouse now and then, for the outhouse or the barn or corrals. Nothing else happened.

"Let's go," Daryl said restlessly. "It's dead down there."

Jessica shook her head. "As you said, they're still awake."

"Playing poker in the bunkhouse," Daryl retorted. "So what? Why are you and Ki so determined to keep tabs on Cap'n Ryker?"

"Because he's been lying through his pearly teeth."

"C'mon, Jessie, I know you're competitors, but—"

"It's because we're competitors that I know he's lying. Listen, Ryker's been saying he's here to consolidate your ranches into one big operation. Well, if he had enough legitimate money to swing such a big package, he'd send representatives and agents to deal for him."

"So he likes to handle it all himself."

"Daryl, does Ryker look like the kind of man who'd come out here if he could avoid it? No. And the only reason he'd have to do it himself is if his finances are so shady and his reasons so sneaky that he can't afford the risk of hirelings finding out. He wants the land, Daryl, I don't question that, but his fancy story about Acme needing beef is only a cover to hide his real motive."

"Which is?"

"That," Jessie sighed, "is why we're waiting."

Abruptly they stiffened, hearing the faint beat of horses hooves echoing hollowly from the pass. More lights began glittering in the Block-Two-Dot buildings, and crewmen from the bunkhouse came out into the yard. Ki stared into the darkness toward the pass.

"Riders," he said.

Jessica kept her eyes on the ranch house. Only two windows were showing any light at all, one being where a front sitting room would be, and the other at the side, in what appeared to be a relatively new addition tacked on to the existing structure. Ryker's office? It was impossible to tell. The window was draped, allowing only a thin crease of lamplight to filter through.

Six or seven riders streamed out of the pass and along the wagon road, reining in when they reached the yard, the bunkhouse hands closing to meet them. Ryker's big bulk was silhouetted in the ranch house doorway as he stepped outside. The men clustered around him for a short while, and Jessica wished she could somehow be down there to overhear the conversation.

Ryker disappeared back into the house. There was more activity in the yard as some of the bunkhouse crew saddled horses and, together with the riders, galloped out of the yard. Hoofbeats drummed loudly and then receded as the men vanished back along the road and up into the pass. Quiet descended across the ranch again, the remaining hands returning to the bunkhouse and closing its door.

Daryl rubbed his ear. "Wonder what that was about."

"Suppose I told you those were the rustlers?"

"No!" Daryl gasped, stiffening. "Jessie, are you sure?"

"Like I keep trying to tell you, Daryl," she replied irritably, "I *think* I have some of the answer to what's been going on hereabouts, and I *think* more of the answer is down at that ranch. But the only thing I *know* right now is that I can't be sure of anything yet."

"But—but if you're right, then we've got to go warn—"

"Warn who? Which rancher, Daryl? And by the time we could follow that bunch to wherever they're raiding, and then get help, they'd have struck and moved on. Relax, Daryl, we're waiting."

79

Shortly, the lamp in the sitting room winked out, followed by another one being briefly lit at the far end of the house, presumably in a bedroom; Ryker was getting ready for bed. Fifteen minutes later, the lamp in the study was snuffed, and the entire ranch house was now dark, silent, undisturbed. Jessica hesitated for a while longer, but nothing suspicious occurred.

"All right, let's give it a whirl," Jessica said, moving away from the edge. "I figure Ryker's had time enough to fall asleep."

"But the men in the bunkhouse," Daryl protested. "I know there ain't many of them there now, but they're all still awake."

She smiled tautly, "Why, they're busy at poker, remember?"

As they hurried to their horses, Jessica was glad to stretch her cramped muscles. Worming back down the steep, narrow crevice was ticklish business, but at last they reached the base of the cliff and cautiously began to approach the ranch.

Coming to a small clump of trees at the extreme edge of the yard, Ki reined in and said in a low voice, "We'll walk from here."

They dismounted and ground-hitched their horses, and Jessica whispered to Daryl, "You stay here and guard them for us."

"Not on your tintype," he declared adamantly.

"Daryl, you wouldn't have gotten this far," Jessica snapped crossly, "except you insisted on jumping into things you don't know anything about."

"And you don't either," he reminded her. Stooping, he tugged off his boots; his socks had holes in them, but he ignored his bare toes sticking out, adding, "My feet are tougher'n rawhide, and when it comes to creeping around, the only one quieter'n me might be Ki, in those slipper-shoes of his."

Jessica turned to Ki for support, but Ki only shrugged, a slightly amused expression on his face. Grudgingly she gave up arguing, realizing Daryl could be just as stubborn as she was, and together the three glided from the trees and crossed into the yard.

Reaching the near corner of the first outbuilding, they paused and listened, checking every shadow for the presence of a guard. They had seen none from the rock, but this was not the time or place to rely on assumptions. Again, they saw no sign of one.

From the outbuilding, they cut swiftly through the yard, making a wide circuit around the bunkhouse. They melted into the night beyond the corral, then eased back toward the ranch-house.

They stopped just under the short overhang of the rear porch. Again they strained to hear, to peer into the blackness around them. A coarse laugh sounded from the bunkhouse; a horse in the corral snorted and stamped. Satisfied, Jessica rubbed her palm along the butt of her holstered revolver, and nodded to Ki. Ki took a skeleton key and a thin, pliant strip of metal from his vest and, squatting, went to work on the porch door. A moment later, the latch snicked back, and he warily pushed open the door.

They slipped inside and stood in a dark pantryway, listening, gaining their bearings, before padding into the kitchen beyond. They passed through the kitchen by the glow of the banked fire in the large cast-iron stove, and entered a dining room with an oak table capable of seating a platoon, with elbow space to spare.

At the other end of the dining room were double doors, luckily unlocked. Ki inched one open and they squeezed through into a sitting room. Near the single window was the wide front door, and opposite was a stubby corridor and an inner door, which she surmised led to Ryker's bedroom. Straight ahead, therefore, would be the new wing containing his study.

Breathlessly they crossed between the front door and hallway, fearing their footfalls might be audible. Jessica hesitated before continuing, bird-dogged by apprehensions, even though they heard nothing. Nothing at all...

That was what concerned her—hearing nothing at all.

They crept onward nonetheless, through a succession of smaller rooms, pausing before entering each one to assure themselves of unobserved passage. Finally they arrived at the study door. This too was closed and locked. Swiftly, Ki picked the lock and pushed, hearing from its other side the rattle of a key in its escutcheon. They waited. All remained silent. Ki gradually eased the door wider, until there was room for them to dart into the study.

The study was black, save for a trickle of pale moonlight around the edges of the poorly drawn drapes. Jessica immediately went over, rearranging the drapes so they completely blanketed the study's small-paned window, while Ki lit a small reading lamp and Daryl gently closed and relocked the door.

Most of the study was taken up by a massive six-foot curtain desk, made of quarter-sawn golden oak, with sycamore inlays and pigeonhole cases. It rested with its matching swivel chair on an Oriental carpet, and was surrounded by walls of bookshelves that were crammed with leatherbound books and looseleaf folders.

"What're we looking for?" Daryl murmured.

Jessica shrugged, and started poking into drawers and pigeonholes, while Ki began sifting through the material on the shelves. She unearthed very little useful information, other than a curious letter postmarked from Washington, D.C.:

My dear Guthried:

I trust you're finding life among the savages and cutthroats not overly unbearable. Your endurance will be well rewarded, I assure you, and this is to confirm that I've already taken steps to arrange for five percent of the stock to be issued in your name. Of course, this is predicated on your success in purchasing all the land we require, and the subsequent merger of Acme with our new corporation. I'm also pleased to report that we've decided on the name of American Federated Development, which has a nice solid ring to it, I believe, without meaning anything. As soon as I receive your wire, I shall introduce my bill and guide it through to passage.

Yours respectfully,
Dilworth Trumbull

Jessica pocketed the letter, frowning as she tried to remember precisely who Dilworth Trumbell was. A congressman, obviously, but—

"Jessie," Ki hissed, interrupting her thoughts. "Come here and take a look at this, see what you make of it."

Jessica and Daryl crossed to where Ki stood by one bookcase, his hands holding wide an unfurled surveyor's section map of Wyoming Territory. A red ink line had been drawn along the same hazardous trail Jessica and Ki had traveled from Uva to Eucher Butte, apparently indicating where an improved road was to be built. Another line ran in a haphazard wriggle from Eucher Butte north to the site of Fort Fetterman, then west and down to just below Casper, then south to intersect the Little Medicine Bow River, and then back across the Eucher Butte. Roughly estimated, the box-like shape it formed encompassed some 3,700 square miles of territory.

"Unbelievable," Daryl gasped. "He's buying all that?"

"I guess so," Jessica whispered. "Trying to, anyway."

"He's already bought or optioned some of it," Ki added, indicating where, within the box, blocks of property had been marked with X's. "And hardly any of it is good as range or farmland."

Daryl shook his head in amazement. "Whatever Ryker wants it for, it'll be the largest land-grab since we revolutioned from the British—"

A moan cut him off, freezing all three of them. It was a low, muffled sound coming from somewhere nearby, and when, after a long moment, they didn't hear the groan again,

Ki rerolled the map and picked up the lamp, whispering, "I'll go out first."

"Wait," Jessica cautioned. "Cast some light around. I swear that moan didn't come from inside the house—or outside, either."

Ki held the lamp higher, so that its feeble glow could better illuminate the dark nooks and crannies. At first nothing appeared out of the ordinary, until the study, concealed in an easily overlooked corner where two bookcases met, was reflected the outline of a small inset door.

On a wild impulse, Jessica went to the door, her saner self rebelling even as she eased down on its handle. The door opened against her gentle pressure. She peered down a short flight of stairs to a basement landing, glimpsing a dim finger of light lancing from somewhere farther back. And wafting up came the familiar odor of a wine cellar— that distinct blend of tannin, cork, and mold, which woke in Jessica's memory the many genial excursions she'd taken with her father's servants, when hunting bottles for dinner in the cellars of the Circle Star ranch.

"Shut the door," Daryl pleaded. "It's only a wine—"

There rose from the basement another moan, longer this time, with a clearly pleading tone to it, as though someone was being tortured.

"Oh, no, it's not," Jessica whispered back to Daryl. "It's another Ryker lie, another trick to cover up something wretched."

Hesitating only long enough for Ki to move ahead with the lamp, Jessica followed him down the steps, Daryl trailing reluctantly, gripping his old Remington revolver. At the bottom stretched two rows of bottles stacked in ceiling-high tiers, and the finger of light she'd seen from upstairs was emanating from a half-open door at the end of this corridor. The bottles, the tiers, the cellar itself were all quite new, Jessica observed, probably dating from the same time as the addition of the study to the main house above.

Moving between the rows toward the door, Jessica rationalized her reckless urge by arguing that the more she learned about her enemies, the more effectively she could defeat them. And for starters, she wanted to find out who was moaning and why, and if it had anything to do for the reason behind the cellar's existence. That it was a ruse, a blind to disguise some other purpose, was clear to her; no host in his right mind would build a wine cellar so far from the dining room.

Reaching the end of the tiers, they saw that the door was in a plank wall that partitioned the rear of the cellar into a separate room. Open to view through the widely ajar door, the room was brightly lit by a library lamp hanging from a ceiling joist. Its floor was matted with straw, and its walls were thickly padded with canvas quilting; spaced around the room were big wooden blocks carved out in places to fit the shape of the human body, with leather thongs and belts, and innumerable chains dangling from their fronts and sides.

A woman was shackled to one of the blocks. She was on the good side of forty, Jessica judged, with black hair to her waist, pendulous breasts, and large quivering thighs. She was entirely naked, except for leather sandals and metal-studded leather cuffs at her wrists, to which the chains were padlocked. Her lips, breasts, and loins were painted to accentuate her sexuality, and her eyes were treated with mascara to look twice their normal size. And from her neck to her knees, her flesh was a mass of lacerations, new redder welts laid crisscrossing over older pink scars.

Guthried Ryker was similarly naked, except for a leather belt heavily studded with iron, which he wore around his pudgy waist. He also had on sandals, but instead of leather cuffs, he wore gauntlets. He was patently aroused, his erection jutting like a ship's boom from his hairy groin. And held in his right hand, slapping lightly against his leg, was a vicious cat-o'-nine-tails.

Sensing an intrusion, Ryker wheeled to face the group in the doorway. His pursy mouth gaped open, and instinctively his right hand made a slight whipping motion with the tails, which he instantly checked. Ki remained still, guardedly poised. Daryl stared dumbfounded, his revolver pointing downward. Jessica glowered rigidly, infuriated and disgusted.

"What are *you* doing here?" Ryker snarled.

"What are you *doing* here?" Daryl blurted in shock.

Ryker blinked, then chuckled throatily. "Why, just a little recreation, m'boy. A little stirring of the blood to relax me."

"Release her," Ki said, coldly but calmly.

"Come now, let's not be naïve about this. My friend is being well paid for her pain." Ryker moved almost imperceptively into a crouch, adding: "And I do believe Dolores enjoys it, too."

"I'm sure Trumbull will enjoy it, when I write him," Jessica retorted with poisoned sweetness. "I'm sure he'll be delighted to share this with the other stockholders of American Federated."

She had no intention of writing Dilworth Trumbull or anyone else; her threat was merely to throw Ryker off his stride, and see what came of it. Nothing did, at first. Ryker showed no alarm, no fear, only a deep surprise. A tense silence gripped the room.

Then, with the suddenness and speed of a striking snake, Ryker's hand shot back the tails and snapped them forward. Jessica had no time or space in which to avoid the blow, so she caught the full blow of the lashes across her breasts and belly. It felt like a shatter of glass in the skin, in the sensitive lair of flesh beneath—it was not one redhot sting of fire, but a general cracking agony that caused her to shudder, screaming.

But even before Ryker could complete the arc of his swing, Ki had released one of his *shuriken* throwing blades from the sheath strapped to his arm under his shirt. The spinning, razon-sharp star glinted in the lamplight as it left his fingers. And simultaneously, Daryl raised his revolver and triggered.

The .44-40 bullet hit a split second before the *shuriken*. Daryl's hasty shot blew most of Ryker's left ear off. Ryker howled, clapping his left hand to the stump of his ear, toppling back and to one side. It wasn't until he'd bumped into the block where the woman was chained that he noticed Ki's *shuriken* embedded in his right shoulder, close to his neck. If he hadn't jerked off balance when first struck by Daryl's heavy lead slug, the *shuriken* would have sliced into his throat and killed him instantly.

"Goddamn you!" he bawled, still falling against the block, sending it and the woman over with him as he crashed to the floor. The woman was shrieking now, struggling futilely in her chains, kicking out and managing accidently to catch him in the groin with one sandal. Which pretty well took care of his withering erection, and any other notion of resistance he might have had. The cat-o'-nine-tails dropped from his nerveless fingers, and with eyes filming and legs turning to jelly, Ryker collapsed, unconscious, on the straw.

"Let's move," Jessie snapped, moving from the door. "Fast!"

Daryl hesitated, bewildered. "But that lady in there—"

"We don't have the time, the keys, or a way to take her if we could get her loose," Ki yelled, propelling Daryl along between the rows of bottles. "What we've got are your poker-playing pals from the bunkhouse, doubtless coming fast after hearing your shot!"

★

Chapter 8

Up the stairs to the study they raced, then through the ranch house, back to the pantry. They reached the rear door just as the crew from the bunkhouse came rushing in across the yard.

Both Jessica and Daryl had their revolvers leveled, when they and Ki stepped out. The half-dozen men hauled up short, their own pistols drawn, pointing every which way but the right way.

"Far enough," Daryl ordered. "Toss your guns away."

The crew milled indecisively, stymied by the two revolvers aiming straight at them. Then, one by one, they gave in, throwing their weapons off into the darkness. Eyeing them warily, Jessica, Ki, and Daryl moved off the porch and began edging around toward the side of the yard where, beyond, they'd posted their horses.

"Your boss isn't dead," Jessica told the crew, her large-framed .38 never wavering in her fist. "Fact is, he's down in the wine cellar, way in the rear, waiting for you boys."

They continued backing away from the disarmed group, and were almost to the corner of the first outbuilding again when they stiffened, listening. Hoofbeats sounded in increasing tempo, heading along the road from the pass, directly for the yard.

"Hot damn!" one of the gang cried. "They're coming back!"

"Yeah, we've got this bunch trapped!"

It was true. The three could hear the riders sweeping in toward the ranch behind them, and the men they were covering were regaining their nerve, already scrambling for their thrown pistols.

Jessica, Ki and Daryl pivoted as one, and started running for the protection of the outbuilding's shadows. "Get them!" they heard a raspy voice shout, and the bunkhouse crew, finding their weapons, began firing eagerly in their direction.

When they came to the back of the outbuilding, Daryl swiveled and his Remington spat flame. A man dropped and another cursed. Joining Daryl, Jessica fired with deadly precision, scattering the initial charge of Ryker's men, downing two more. Thundering battle broke loose in the yard, pistols bucking, lead searching.

In the dark, bloody confusion, the trio managed to run in a crouch away from the outbuilding. They streaked, ducking and zigzagging, to the edge of the yard, then cut toward the grove where their horses were waiting. They knew they had a bare minute before the approaching riders would descend and spread out hunting for them—and in that minute they'd have to be gone, or be dead.

They were merely flitting silhouettes in the field between the yard and the trees, when the riders galloped in. A quick, shouting uproar and the blood-cry of pursuit rose from the yard, and the riders turned, roweling their mounts toward the fleeing trio.

They dove into the trees, Jessica and Daryl holstering

their pistols as they all grabbed reins and leaped for saddles. "'Bye, boots," Daryl said regretfully as they wheeled their horses away from the Block-Two-Dot. Then, breaking from the grove, he shouted, "It's a race for it! Head for the pass!"

They bent over their horses' withers, and the animals chewed up the ground. Shots snarled after them, but the swaying riders behind them couldn't aim effectively, their bullets off target, high and wild. They didn't bother to return the fire. It would be nip-and-tuck all the way to the pass.

The earth blurred under pounding hoofs. The rolling beat of pursuing horses echoed loud and thundering. The pass was an eternity away. The fusillade of avenging lead buzzed close by their heads.

The murky slopes of the hills loomed closer, and finally they could see the black maw of the pass. Jessica risked a quick glance behind her. She could plainly hear the onrushing riders, but could only make them out as a group bunched together in the hazy darkness. From her brief glimpse of their bulk, however, she estimated they were just the bunkhouse crew, and not the combined force.

At last they plunged into the narrow pass, Daryl slightly in the lead, urging his buckskin to greater speed. Short moments later, the towering walls of the pass echoed as the pursuers swept in after them along the rutted trail. The chase continued, the pass gradually rising and blending into the foothills and opening out into a draw. Beyond, a wide rock-strewn plateau extended to another maze of night-heavy ridges and canyons. Naked of trees, the plateau gleamed under moonlight, which made pearls of the stones littering their path.

The three rode hard across the flat. The only sounds were the deep panting of the horses, and their drumming strides against the rocky soil—and the faint rataplan of hoofbeats coming after them.

"Ryker's boys still have us in sight," Jessica said loudly.

"Not for long," Daryl shouted back. "They're going to wind up chasing their tails all night, when I get done confusing them. Nobody 'cept my dad knows these hills better'n I do."

Reaching the edge of the plateau, Daryl began skirting a twisted ravine, gesturing toward a side trail some distance ahead. Jessica and Ki veered to the left, following him as he swung onto a barely visible track at a dead run. A canyon embraced them, shrinking to a sinuous gorge of solid stone that reverberated with their passage.

Daryl slowed his buckskin and motioned for Jessica and Ki to do the same. Their huffing bays were glad to oblige. They moved on along the granite floor, their easy lope giving off very little noise that could be traced. Behind, the sounds of galloping horses echoed off the rock as the Block-Two-Dot crew entered the canyon.

"Haven't lost them yet," Ki said, glancing back.

"We will," Daryl replied confidently. "Thing is, I don't want them to be able to hear when and where we cut off. It's up a ways—"

"Wait," Jessica interrupted. "Listen."

The two men tensed, straining to catch what she was hearing. Then, from ahead, faint at first, but growing swiftly, rose a deep, earth-trembling roar. Still riding at a loping pace, they became increasingly alarmed the farther they went along the snaky gorge. But they couldn't stop or go back, because of the pursuing riders; they couldn't turn aside, because of the steep slopes and flanking boulders on both edges; they could only continue heading toward the rolling, pounding, fast-approaching tumult.

A few rags of clouds shuttled across high stars, blown by a rush of wind from the north. They caught the moon, released it again; and as the pale light trickled back into the gorge, the trio rounded a sharp bend and faced a looming herd of cattle.

Hastily they reined in, aghast at the sight of this brown wall bearing down on them heads tossing, eyes rolling, horns clacking. It was not a big herd, but it didn't need to be, squeezed as it was within the narrow gully. It was being driven at a rapid clip by punchers on horseback outlined against the starry sky, their prodding shouts lifting above the drubbing beat of hoofs. A little in front trotted one curly-horned, wall-eyed steer that seemed to be the leader.

"I know that brute!" Daryl yelped. "Them're *my* cows!"

"You can have them!" Ki retorted. "Back! Quick!"

His voice was drowned in the deafening roar, but Jessica and Daryl saw him wheel and start heading back the way they'd come. They wrenched their horses around to follow, Daryl's buckskin kicking and plunging, Jessica's bay dancing, ears laid back and eyes wild.

Fear was in the air, fear of this mass of flesh closing inexorably, no more to be halted than a tornado. To yell and wave would be futile; to shoot would be like damming a flood with loose rocks, and could easily result in panic, spooking the steers into stampeding in the only direction they could go—straight ahead.

The dark trail blurred under their horses, their pace too swift for talk, and none was needed. Each could sense the tension and dread in the others, as they galloped around another tight curve, and surged directly toward the oncoming Block-Two-Dot gunhands.

The crew were caught by surprise, but not so much that they didn't react. Predictably, they spurred their horses on, whooping with certain victory, their pistols spurting flame and lead. At such dead-on range, Jessica, Ki and Daryl should have been riddled, but in firing from speeding horses into night shadows, the crew's aim proved inaccurate. Bullets ricocheted off the boulders and whistled past their bodies uncomfortably close, one searing along Daryl's ribs in a long gash. But they continued their suicidal charge, figuring their only chance was to somehow break through the line of gunmen and return to the plateau.

And then the herd came lumbering around the curve.

The gorge abruptly erupted in howling, rattling confusion, the Block-Two-Dot crew shouting in shock and fear, trying to check their horses and spin them about. Some went down as their horses slipped and fell on the shale. Others windmilled arms and hats in a vain attempt to stop the front. Still others, the really stupid ones, turned their fire from the three riders to the crowding steers beyond.

The cattle spooked. Lowing and snorting, they began picking up speed, and as one would stumble or drop with a bullet, the other would leap the barrier and stream on even faster. More gunfire peppered the advancing herd as the crew splintered frenziedly, a few retreating, most of them still attempting to stave off the stampede.

A panic-triggered slug caught Ki's horse in its breastbone. The bay reared with the impact, causing Ki to lurch half out of his saddle, his balance lost. Frantically he grabbed for the saddlehorn, missing it, and started falling headfirst as the horse folded beneath him.

He wriggled clear. Jolting agony jarred through him as he struck the ground, the bay tumbling on its side, its hooves slashing close to his face.

"Ki!" Jessica pivoted her horse toward him, heedless of the oncoming stampede. The curly-horned leader dashed bellowing past her, other steers thronging right behind, and it was almost more than Jessica could do to maneuver her horse out of their path. Daryl, spotting her, swung his buckskin in an arc to intercept her, as the rush of steers surged perilously around him in an increasing tide.

They saw Ki rise, then begin bobbing and weaving in a desperate effort to reach the boulders at the nearest side of the trail. "Leave me!" they heard him cry as he dove among the swelling torrent of hoofs and horns. "Save yourselves—or we'll all die!"

Jessica ignored his plea and made a last convulsive try, struggling against the flow of crazed cattle to save him. But that shoving melee flung her back as easily as a baby. She reeled, tilting far off balance, and the flinty tip of a longhorn snagged her jacket, tearing through it and her shirt, gouging a burning furrow diagonally across her side and back. She would have lost control, had not Daryl swerved alongside and grabbed the cheekstrap of her horse's bridle, pulling the animal around in line with the maddened herd.

"No!" Eyes wide, face chalky white, Jessica fought to stop him. "Let me go, Daryl, we can't leave Ki—"

"Dammit, we have no choice!"

They were swept along shoulder to shoulder with the steers, shoulder to shoulder with sudden death, but at least they were going in the right direction. The Block-Two-Dot crew was not. Men fell, horses tripped, and the stampede crushed them in its relentless pressure, trampling and slashing them under sharp hooves. The agonized cries of the injured and dying were faint in the overwhelming, thunderous maelstrom.

And the avalanche of beef rolled implacably on toward the plateau, moonlight glinting on tossing backs and piercing horns. Carried along in the hemming current, Jessie and Daryl could hear the bellowing of frightened animals and the pounding of hooves drumming the stony trail. This was no place for a poor rider, or for a coward.

The gorge widened into the short stretch of canyon, and from the canyon the herd funneled out, spreading across the plateau. Daryl angled for a narrow crevice at one side of the canyon mouth, Jessica followed, slumped in her saddle. The herd kept plummeting past in a swirl of dust and horns and hooves, not a dozen yards from the spot where they hid.

Eventually the drag drained through, the rustlers behind them yelling and cursing as they tried to stem the runaway, paying no attention to the narrow crevice. Watching them, Daryl commented disgustedly, "They'll never turn them. By morning, my cows will be scattered from hell to breakfast out there in the brakes."

"We've got to go back," Jessica said dully.

"We can't."

"We can't leave Ki!"

"We have to." Daryl turned, leaning across to wrap a comforting arm around her, being careful not to press her bleeding wound. "Listen, Jessie, I know how you feel, but you've got to understand. Maybe half the gang chasing us wasn't skinned or stomped, and they're still back there, sorer than kerosened snakes. We couldn't go looking for Ki, or stop to help him if we found him."

"But he could be hurt, or . . . dead."

"If he's dead, he's dead, and getting ourselves shot won't make him alive. If he's hurt, he's got a better chance of living by lying low, staying put, instead of us drawing attention to him."

"Tomorrow . . ."

"Sure, Jessie, tomorrow. We'll come back for him tomorrow, but right now, tonight, it's more important to take care of you."

★

Chapter 9

They rode in silence through the murky hills, hearing the bawling of cattle and the shouting of rustlers receding behind them.

Jessica hunched despondently in the saddle. Daryl was beside her and a bit ahead, leading the way back to the Spraddled M. As they dipped down across a fingerling valley, he noticed on the right a craggy outcropping. Bluestem grass appeared to be growing in foot-high tufts there, an indication of a spring or brook. He pulled alongside Jessica, gesturing, and angled toward the boulders. She headed after him, the horses speeding up as they smelled water.

The outcropping proved to encircle a small patch of bottom, with a thin trickle of water oozing from the ground. A few small animals fled as they approached, but otherwise the area seemed deserted. They dismounted, stiff and exhausted, and knelt in the grass, cupping their hands to drink. The horses lapped thirstily.

"Well, we lost them this time," Jessica said with irony.

"We better have. The horses are too tired for any more fancy prancing. We should give them a short breather."

She nodded wearily. "No argument from me."

Leaving the saddles on, they picketed the horses by the water and went to the outcropping, where the grass was dryer. Jessica sucked in her breath, grimacing from pain, as she slowly sat down. Frowning, Daryl hunkered beside her and tentatively touched her back.

"Bend forward a tad," he said. "If you can."

She leaned over, biting her lip to stifle a moan, feeling him gently peel away the ripped fabric that was stuck to her coagulating blood. The long gash opened up again, a line of warm moistness seeping out and rivuleting down her back.

"Doesn't look too deep," Daryl said, still frowning with concern. "My guess is, with a cleaning and bandaging and a good smear of ointment, your cut should heal up right fine."

She tried to make light of it. "Nary a scar, doctor?"

"Probably not, if we treat it right soon. I ain't any doc, though; I'm just going by how I tend my cows."

Shortly they were up and riding again, across the range of wooded slopes, stony ridges, and brushy draws. Jessica fell to following Daryl again, more than willing to let him find their way through. He did, competently. And as fatigued and aching as she was, Jessica made sure to memorize the route he took.

When they cleared the hills and entered his ranch yard, the buildings dozed dark and still, appearing abandoned, as if the rustlers had not only made off with a small bunch of Spraddled M stock, but with all the hands as well.

Inside the house, Daryl lit a glass stand lamp and ushered Jessica into the kitchen. "Stay here," he said, and then made two trips outside, one for wood with which to stoke the cast-iron Duchess stove, and the other for water to fill the washtub he placed on the stove's burners. While the water was heating, he hauled out a heavy tin bathtub, and placed it near the stove.

"This ain't the height of modesty," he said, beginning to redden around the ears. "But I reckon it'll just have to do."

"I'll manage nicely, thank you," Jessica replied, managing to keep a serious expression. She trailed him into an adjacent bedroom, saying, "Bad as it was, we learned a lot tonight."

"Sure did." His back was to her as he ransacked a tall wardrobe. "Now, I know I've got a clean towel in here somewheres."

"We learned that Ryker wants a big chunk of Wyoming for no good reason, and that in order to get it, he's resorting to rustling."

"The one don't mean the other. Ah, here're a couple."

"Yes, it does. When we ran into those steers—your steers—they were being herded toward the Block-Two-Dot, weren't they?"

"Yeah, along that rocky gorge. No wonder Deputy Oakes could never find no tracks," Daryl said, as they returned to the kitchen. "I'll use this one for freshenin'. Here, you take the bigger one."

The bigger towel was the size of a child's blanket. Jessica refolded it and laid it on the kitchen table, continuing, "And I'll bet you anything that the men who were herding them are the same men we saw earlier—that first bunch who rode into the Block-Two-Dot yard, and then rode off again with some of the bunkhouse crew."

"Okay, so supposing there is a connection. But why? Ryker don't need more stock; he already owns more'n his range can handle."

"Daryl, Ryker isn't a rancher like the rest of you, struggling to make ends meet, hoping to build a future. He's a crook, tied in with a whole ring of bigger crooks who'll stop at nothing to gain control of that block of land we saw on that map. It follows like night follows day that he's using the rustlers to cripple you ranchers, as a wedge to buy you up for nickels and force you off your property."

Daryl brooded for a moment, then stepped closer, searching her eyes. "Jessie, you'd best leave Eucher Butte as soon as you can."

"Leave? I don't want to leave, I want to stay."

"I want you to stay too, of course, but you must leave, for your own sake. I won't have you dying for a fight that isn't yours."

"This *is* my fight, Daryl. More than you know."

"You've already done as much as any man could. More!" He gripped her tenderly by the shoulders. "But if you're right, and in my gut I know you are, then Ryker and these other crooks won't stop at nothing. They sure won't stop at brutalizing or killing a woman."

"And what about . . . about Ki?" she asked, faltering, a lump gathering in her throat. "We made it our fight when we came in answer to Mrs. Waldemar's letter, and now that Ki is missing, I won't rest—I *cannot* rest—until I finish the fight we started together."

Daryl heard her sob, as she pressed her cheek against his chest. It seemed so natural for her to melt in his arms, as natural as lowering his face to kiss her, the pressure of her body like an eager promise. Shaken and chagrined, Daryl released her, taking a step backwards. "F-forgive me, Jessica, I didn't mean to be forward."

Jessica looked as though she weren't paying the slightest attention to his apology. She placed the open palm of one hand flat against his cheek. "You need a shave," she said, stroking upward against the stubble. "When I rub down, it's smooth, and when I rub up, you're all whiskers."

Daryl shivered, speechless from her caress, staring at her affectionate smile. There were rents in her clothes, and one sleeve of her plaid shirt was almost torn away. Bloodstains and scratches marred her smooth, tanned face and delicate hands, and her long hair, tangled and hatless, gleamed like the hue of fireweed honey where the glowing fire from the stove reflected against it. She was a lovely thing, and Daryl battled hard to retain his control.

"The, ah, the water is warm," he finally managed, blushing to his hairline. "We...I mean, you can have a nice bath now."

Hastily he poured the steaming water into the plunge-tub, leaving a little in the washtub for his own use. He tossed her a cake of soap, grabbed another and his towel, and fled with the washtub into the front room. "Soak as long as you like," he called.

"I will," she replied lightly, shedding her clothes in a pool on the kitchen floor. "But Daryl...I expect you to shave."

A throat-clearing sounded from the other room, causing her to broaden her smile as she eased naked into the bath water. She washed carefully, thoroughly, wanting to be squeaky clean in case anything developed—which, considering Daryl's flustered behavior, was not entirely impossible.

She was not in the habit of seducing men, although occasionally she enjoyed a bit of coy flirting; it was a pleasing game, and it gratified her to know she could arouse the stuffiest, most virtuous of males on a basic, primitive level. Nor was she a promiscuous wanton, the victim of some insatiable sex drive. It was simply that Jessica Starbuck was not a prude or a hypocrite; she was pure woman, proud of her femininity, and she relished the sensation of being attractive to those few men she found desirable.

And Lord, Daryl Melville was desirable! She had thought so ever since their first meeting, and thinking of him now caused her taut breasts to tingle, her rosy nipples to harden involuntarily. Daryl possessed a rare allure that seemed to captivate and fascinate her, to bore to the very essence of her sensual nature. The easy grace of his motions, the strong muscles flexing along his thighs and chest, the hard bas-relief of his loins in his pants...

Whoops! Jessica straightened in the tub, chastising herself. It was one thing to admire him, or even to desire him; it was quite another to get herself worked into a frazzle.

She stepped out of the tub, dripping water and trying to wrap the large towel around her. "Are you decent, Daryl?"

"Yes."

"Well, don't peek. I'm having trouble with this towel of yours." She sauntered into the front room, the towel perversely slipping and unraveling, no matter how she tried to hold it closed.

Daryl ignored her warning, naturally. He was standing in front of the fireplace, shaving by the reflection of the large mantelpiece mirror. He was barefoot and shirtless, wearing only his trousers, and Jessica could see the muscular power of his naked torso as he stroked his cheek with a straight razor.

She also saw him nearly slice an ear off, when he took a look at her, bare-breasted. Hastily, Jessica struggled to raise the hem of the towel back over her bosom. Which she managed to do, but at the cost of one edge of the towel behind her parting like an errant stage curtain and fully, if briefly, exposing her firm buttocks and lithely tapering thighs.

The razor dropped to the floor.

Jessica retreated, scampering. "I said not to peek!"

"I didn't see a thing, Jessie. Honest!" There was a pause, then Daryl asked, "Was there something you wanted?"

"Well, you told me my cut needs ointment and bandages, and I can't very well reach all the way around my back and do it, can I?"

"Oh." There was another pause, longer and somehow more profound. Then, nervously: "I, ah, I'll do it. You go get arranged on my bed, and I'll be in as soon's I finish here."

In the bedroom, Jessica stretched out on her stomach on the iron-framed single bed, and very carefully made sure the towel was draped properly over her from the waist down.

Mentally she kicked herself, flaming with embarrassment, for that impromptu strip-tease with the towel had been truly accidental, and not like her at all.

Daryl entered, clearing his throat a lot, and put a roll of adhesive tape, some gauze bandages, scissors, and a tin of ointment on the bedside table. He sat down, balancing on the edge of the bed with all the caution of a man expecting the mattress to explode.

"Just consider me one of your cows," Jessica said, hoping to relax him, her face buried in the covers. "I'll moo, if it'll help."

With a tight chuckle, Daryl opened the tin and began to spread the ointment hesitantly along her wound. It burned like a branding iron.

"My god, Daryl, what is that stuff? Acid?"

"Arnicated carbolic salve," he answered, pausing to quote the label: "'The best in the world for burns, flesh injuries, boils, eczema, chilblains, piles, ulcers, and fever sores.'" He started smoothing it on again, assuring her, "Dad swears by it for his salt rheum and ringworm. Don't worry, it'll smart for just a minute, and then it'll just feel nice warm."

Jessica lay still, skeptically waiting for the salve to stop burning and start warming. Amazingly it did, the warmth penetrating while Daryl continued rubbing gingerly with his fingers. He leaned over her back, so close that she could feel his breath against her flesh and smell the fragrance of his masculine body . . . and gradually, against her will, she sensed budding tendrils of pleasure beginning to curl deep down in her belly and loins and gently clenching buttocks.

"Jessie . . . ?"

"Mm?"

"Remember Ryker's cellar? His chains and whips?"

"Mm."

"Does that kind of thing . . . do girls go for that?"

"A few, maybe. Me, I'm strictly a soft touch."

Daryl touched her softly. Massaging, kneading, his hands

eased from where the wound started high on one side, down along her spine to the dimple of flesh just above the crevice of her tensing buttocks. His fingers explored very slowly, almost fearfully, and she could hear his breath deepening, his pulse quickening. And she could feel her own lungs sucking in air, her blood racing with a fire that flamed through her flesh and goaded her to reckless abandon.

She turned over. A slight twinge of self-consciousness stole through her as she sat up facing him, seeing his eyes roaming heatedly over her naked, thrusting breasts. "You'll make some lucky girl a real fine husband," she teased in a throbbing voice.

His own voice was husky, choking. "I—I'm sorry, Jessie. That's twice now that I've . . . I don't know what's come over me."

"There's nothing to be sorry about." Intimacy crept into her tone, and she touched his arm. "Only to be happy about," she continued in a sultry purr, her other hand pulling the towel aside. "You want me. After all, I'm a woman and you're a man . . ."

His tongue licked his lips to moisten them, as he stared quivering at her delicately molded thighs and golden-fleeced loins. Desire stirred within him, despite his best intentions. Jessica was not for him to take, he told himself; she was offering her love in a moment of anguish, out of grief and hysteria over the loss of her friend Ki, as a desperate effort to forget and drive out her torment. He would not be the cause of her further suffering—he could not be, and live with himself.

"But Jessica, you . . . you're an angel . . ."

"I'm also a beast," she murmured tauntingly, reaching down to unbuckle his belt. "Let me prove it, prove both of us are."

And then Daryl found himself moving, his body responding of its own volition. His fingers fumbled with the buttons, his hips trembling as he rose to slide his pants down, his flesh aching as Jessica ran her hands around his chest and

103

thighs while helping him rid himself of his clothing. Then he was as naked as she, tanned and muscular and admirably masculine.

Daryl joined her on the bed, his mouth coming down on hers. He kissed her and she kissed back, and fire was in their lips. Awkward with passion, he tried to push her flat and enter her from above, but the press of the covers against her wound was too painful for her to accept. Daryl was a solid man, she realized, without a great deal of imagination or experience, and was probably only familiar with the standard position. Well, that was definitely out of the question tonight.

"Daryl," she whispered, "my back."

He reared as if scalded. "Jesus, I'm sorry, we can't—"

"We can." She drew away slightly, just enough so she could turn and crouch on her knees and elbows with her buttocks thrusting up. It was a submissive position many women dislike, the cow-hitch posture, but what with one thing and another, it seemed exceptionally appropriate for the occasion. She stifled an urge to moo, saying, "This is how beasts do it, isn't it?"

Daryl was eagerly game to try playing the beast. He slid behind her on his knees and took her gently, his hands gliding along her sides and up around to fondle her breasts. He moved deep within her, and Jessica felt him clearly, with a joy that surged through her. It was this elation that made her anchor her feet against the bed, raising her hips to press up and back to match his passionate thrusts. The world spun in a rainbow of colors, but in reality there was no world for Jessica just then—there was only this throbbing, this pulsing rhythm inside her gripping belly. Together they worked in frenzied ecstasy, until at last they reached sweet release, and he spilled his passion deep inside her while she squeezed around him, shuddering.

Daryl sprawled beside her on the cramped bed, his erection fading, his breathing trembling in her ear. But greater indeed was the fulfillment inside Jessica, the effervescent sensation of contentment and satiation. Stirring, she eased from the bed, reaching back with one hand to retrieve the blanket.

"No," Daryl said, smiling up at her. "No blanket."

"But Daryl," she teased, standing naked beside the bed, "what about your modesty that you were so worried about?"

He laughed. "Too late for that, little heifer."

She sashayed to the doorway, standing there in the warmth from the kitchen stove, feeling no embarrassment at all. She felt pleased and natural, basking in his adoring gaze, admiring in return his openly displayed, handsome body.

He rose on an elbow. "You've got me going in circles, y'know."

"About what?"

"You. Us. This."

Smiling, she parried, "You mean about us having sex?"

"Yeah, in a way. I guess I just won't ever figure women out. A man, now, is pretty straightforward. I like a drink when I'm thirsty, and a steak when I'm hollow inside. I've never been much for the notion that there's just one woman in the world for a man, but all the other women I've met up with before don't seem to agree."

"Then it's simple, Daryl. You've merely met up with a woman who's as straightforward as you, and agrees with you." She crossed to the bed and knelt beside him, and as he put out his hand to caress one of her distended nipples, she whispered: "Have you ever studied sex, the art of making love?"

"In Eucher Butte? I'd be tarred and feathered."

"Well, I've tried to avoid living in the Eucher Buttes of this world. I've lived in a lot of other places, and studied and learned."

"And practiced," Daryl added, his mouth closing around her breast, suckling it as if he were an infant seeking milk.

"Japan, the Far East, Arabia, Europe, ahh . . ." she sighed dreamily. "And I've found that passion and desire never made anyone feel sick or guilty. Only the hate and destructiveness that can be hidden in them will produce sickness and bitter regrets."

Daryl's lips left her breast, and he helped lift her back onto the bed. He was ready again to sample her talents, his erection reviving hard and strong as she stretched out beside him, snuggling affectionately, her legs slightly parted.

"Make it as good as the last time," she whispered.

Daryl ran his hand over the mounds of her breasts and down across her smooth belly to the soft, pulsing warmth below. Jessica moaned, her flesh coming alive to his caresses, and her voice sighed in his ear, urging him to quench the fires kindling in her loins.

He kissed her lips, her cheeks, the tender hollow of her neck. Slipping lower, he darted his tongue across her hardened nipples, then moved it wetly along her abdomen, feeling the satiny skin ripple under his tauntings. Then still lower, his lips probing and exploring as she cried out in ecstatic pleasure. She rolled from side to side while he licked at her inner lips; she whimpered deliriously as her throbbing arousal increased, her fingers entangled in his hair.

The splayed thighs beneath his mouth arched and swiveled. Daryl gave them room. Jessica again stretched out alongside him, but now facing the foot of the bed, her legs still spread wide on either side of his bobbing head. Daryl could feel her hands move from his hair and down along his body, clutching his buttocks, pulling him toward her face. Her tongue began teasing him, dancing like a waterbug on the crown of his erection. Daryl pressed her loins harder against his sucking mouth, and a deep animal sound escaped from his nibbling lips.

From below, between his own wide-stretched legs, Jessica dipped further, licking along his rigid shaft, and then plunging her mouth voraciously on it, swallowing it in a soft clinging pressure. Daryl felt his hips writhing, stirring, swaying, his entire lower body seeming to swim in a vast sea of tense sensation.

Jessica's seemingly disembodied lips, her mouth, her

throat were eating him, trying to draw the whole of him into her yearning flesh. Daryl could distinguish no external detail of touch. Doubtless her teeth were there, nipping gently; her tongue was there, licking and twining; her lips were there, pressing and sucking . . . but no detail was clear, only the combining vacuum of suction drawing all of his vital juices down to his groin.

And in response to her own urgent yearnings, Jessica was pressing her naked body full-length against him, undulating back and forth, around and up, so that the potent force of his own tongue was being drawn deep up inside her sensitive flesh. His head was hot, his mouth working, gasping, and a tumultous eruption was growing, growing in his scrotum . . . and from the way Jessica was reacting, he thought she might also be on the verge of climaxing.

Too soon, he thought, *too soon . . .*

On the verge, on the very crest of his orgasm, Daryl felt Jessica pull away slightly, perfectly timing and tapering off, no more ready to end their ecstasy than he. For a long moment longer her mouth lightly suckled his thickened shaft, her tongue dancing teasingly on its bulbous tip. Then she pivoted up, squatting over him, astride him, knees on the bed on either side of his hips.

She gazed down at him with eyes filmed with passion, and then impaled herself on his spearing erection, contracting her strong inner thighs, her muscular action clamping her moist passage tightly around his shaft. "This one, a knowing Frenchman would call *monde renverse.* You like?"

"I like," Daryl groaned, clenching his buttocks, thrusting his hips up off the covers in greedy response. "Oh, I like . . ."

Jessica splayed her kneeling legs, settling down until she contained all of his rigid, lust-hardened shaft within her. Slowly at first, then with increasing fierceness, she began sliding up and down. This was a posture more to her liking, allowing her to be the dominant partner, freeing her to control the pace and stimulation. Her head sagged, then tautened again in arousal, a vein standing out at the side of her throat with the fury of her pumping exertion. Her mouth o ned and closed in mute testimony to the exquisite sensa ons plundering her loins, her long blonde hair swaying nd brushing down over her shoulders and across his chest.

Daryl grasped her jiggling breasts, toying harshly with them until hoarse moans were drawn from her slackened lips. She bent for a brief moment with a whisper of a kiss, then arched up and back as she plunged deeper, faster, reaching behind to caress Daryl's scrotum, massaging with delicately stroking fingernails. The backward angle made her body toss precariously on Daryl's hips, her thighs descending with building force, only to reverse at the last instant and draw up again on his penetrating shaft.

Daryl, tensing upward, felt the gripping of her sheath tearing at his entrails. "God, Jessica, you're like a vice," he panted.

Her passage kept squeezing, squeezing, as she crooned above him, her mouth open, her eyes wide and sightless. The squeezing grew unbearable until, bursting, Daryl came again.

Jessica's loins worked and sucked as if his juices were some invigorating tonic, to be ravenously swallowed in her belly, as her own face contorted and twisted with spasming climax.

Then, with the ebb of passion, Jessica crouched limp and satiated over Daryl. Slowly, sighing contentedly, she eased off his flaccid body and lay down on the bed alongside him. Daryl felt drugged, unable to move. He wanted to say something, but was at a loss for words. Instead, he silently cradled her in his arms and dozed off, their bodies remaining loosely entwined . . .

Jessica awoke from a restless sleep.

Tensely, she remained quiet beside Daryl, listening to his easy breathing and watching the rhythmic rise and fall of his sweat-slick chest. Then, gradually, gently, she sat up and eased from his lax embrace, slipping noiselessly from the bed.

Cautiously, so as not to disturb him, she took the gauze,

108

the roll of tape, and the pair of scissors, and padded into the kitchen. By the frail glow of the stove's embers, she awkwardly patched her wound and began gathering her clothes. Her jeans and boots were still in fair shape, but her shirt and jacket were virtual rags. She went into the front room and snitched Daryl's heavy cloth workshirt; it fit her like a tent, but at least it was in one whole piece. She wrapped it around her, tucking it in and rolling up the sleeves, then put her ripped jacket on over it. It would have to suffice.

Soundlessly she moved to the front door, boots in hand, and twisted the handle. The hinges squeaked. She hesitated, licking dry lips, glancing fretfully back toward the bedroom.

There was a sound of Daryl fidgeting, but his breathing continued guttural and even. She thought of the angular lines of his naked body stretched out on the covers, and was filled with the desire to strip again and climb back in bed next to him. She fought her temptation, furtively crossing the threshold and closing the door behind her, leaning against it for balance as she tugged on her boots.

It was just before dawn, and a cold, silvery light touched only the jagged rim of the distant hills. Spying the outline of the otherwise murky slopes just increased Jessica's bitter resolve. Swiftly she crossed to the barn where her horse was stalled, and walking the bay out and safely away from the house, she stepped into the saddle and rode west toward the hills.

The dawn had evolved into an overcast morning of melancholy grayness by the time Jessica had retraced Daryl's route back to the rocky gorge. She passed the spot where the Block-Two-Dot crew had been trampled, and saw that most of the men and horses had survived; there were only a few corpses dotted around. Even fewer steers were sprawled lifeless in a short line from there back up the gorge trail, the results of the crew's panicked shooting.

When she located Ki's dead bay, she dismounted and started her search. Ki was not anywhere in open view, which gave her hope—though he could just as readily have been

109

thrown into the boulders, or been injured and crawled out of sight. To die.

"Ki!"

His name echoed mockingly. Grit and pebbles crunched under her boots as Jessica ran along both sides of the trail, calling for him over and over. When she failed to find him at first, she sought him a second and then a third time, up and down the edges, going farther than where they'd encountered the herd, and back to the mouth of the canyon, where she and Daryl had hid.

"Ki!" she continued crying out, her voice rising with growing alarm. Increasingly frantic, she stumbled over and over across the sharp stones, her breath coming short and hurting under her breast.

"Ki!"

There was no answer. Except for the scattered remains from the stampede, Jessica was utterly alone.

★

Chapter 10

Ki, thrown by his dying horse, had scrambled in a frantic dash for the bouldered side of the gorge. He'd whirled and leaped to keep from being trampled, and when he glimpsed Jessica and Daryl struggling to reach him, he had to strain his lungs to be heard. "Save yourselves... or we'll all die..."

Then the stampede rampaged close and enveloped him. A hoof caught him in the shin and almost broke it; he swallowed the pain and plowed on through the churning, trampling herd. The boulders... he could see the boulders... an arm's length away...

And then he saw the maddened longhorn plunging straight for him, head down, horns rolling, nostrils leaving a stream of foam in the moonlight. There wasn't any time to dive out of the way. He could only fling himself flat and let the steer leap over him. As he did so, the stampede and

111

its thunder grew vague and gray, blending into a swirling black fog...

Consciousness returned, along with a staggering headache. Ki lay where he was, propped on one elbow, his thoughts slowly clearing. The steer must have kicked him a glancing blow; luckily it had been a straggler, in the drag of the herd, or else he'd surely have been run over by others. Dazed, holding his head in his hands, Ki sat up and peered groggily around.

The gorge was quiet. Ther herd was gone, the only steers in sight the few dead ones the Block-Two-Dot crew had shot. But facing Ki in a haphazard semicircle were six men in range garb, dirty and sweat-streaked, their expressions hard. He would instantly have perceived them to be some of Ryker's riders—perhaps the only uninjured survivors after their mauling by the herd—even if he hadn't recognized one of them as the ranch ramrod, Volpes. The man was standing back, strangely poised, eyeing Ki as if he were a casual bystander; but the carbine nestled in the crook of Volpes's arm didn't look casual at all.

"Be up in a minute, I said, didn't I?" Volpes grinned and spat. "Always said chinks have cast-iron skulls."

Nobody confirmed or denied it.

"Okay," Volpes said, "grab him and tie him up. The boss'll want this smart turd alive."

The five moved in with more relish than caution.

Ki scrambled upright, his face purposely fearful while he threw up both hands as if in entreaty. But what he expected didn't happen; no *shuriken* sprang from his sleeves to appear in his hands. He flicked his wrists. Still nothing. Jammed! Somehow, with all the grit and banging around, the damned release mechanisms had broken!

Not that the five crewmen were aware of this, of how near to death they had all come, as they sprang for him. Seemingly trapped by their swift convergence, Ki had time for only a *kapalabhati* cleansing breath before embracing their attack—*nukishomen-uchi*—drawing them and himself into the circular harmony of the universe.

112

Ki stunned the nearest man with a back-knuckled "ram's head" jab between the eyes. Without turning, without apparently seeing his target, he stabbed the second with a left-handed thumb-and-forefinger thrust to the throat, constricting the flow of blood through both jugular veins and dropping the man unconscious. Meanwhile, he stopped the man tackling from the rear with a sideways snap-kick; his solar plexus paralyzed, the man sank to his knees, convinced he was dying. But the fourth man managed to come in butting from the other side, knocking Ki just enough off balance so he could gouge his knee in the small of Ki's back and apply a full nelson.

"I got him now! Beat the shit outta him!"

"You betcha!" The fifth man grinned, plunging forward.

Using the man behind him for support, Ki bunched both legs in a flying upward thrust, his heels catching the fifth man square in the balls. The man doubled up, uttering short croaks of agony and confusion.

Then, planting his feet firmly on the ground again, Ki simply backed up. The man behind him, who had both arms and one foot engaged in the lock he had put on Ki, was thrown immediately off balance, and had to remove the knee he'd put in the small of Ki's back, to keep himself from falling. So Ki just relaxed and bent his knees and dropped out from under the full nelson, turning as he did so to deliver an elbow-strike just beneath the fellow's breastbone. The man went down, and Ki was just preparing to finish the job with a heel to the groin, when he felt the press of cold steel against his temple.

"You move," Volpes said coldly, "and I'll blow your fuckin' pigtail brains out."

Slowly, Ki lowered the foot he was planning to stomp with and stood motionless. His face became taut, expressionless, as the rifle continued to bore into his temple.

The five fallen men began stirring, crawling and gasping raggedly, then tottering upright, holding themselves, hacking and wheezing.

"S'mbitch," the one who'd been hit in the balls croaked.

113

He was still in a crouch, one hand cupped over his groin. "The bastard's nailed. C'mon, let's pay him back!"

The men all staggered forward, lunging at Ki. They were big, husky, range-toughened brawlers, used to absorbing a lot of punishment and dishing it back out. Yet it was likely none of them would have been alive, much less standing, if Ki hadn't been caught weakened and groggy, before he'd had a chance to revive his flagging energy. But he had been caught, so the men were standing, crowding in, while Volpes held Ki at bay with his finger tight around the trigger.

The infuriated men surged forward, bent on revenge, arms seizing and fists smashing. Ki stumbled, blinding pain seeming to shatter his skull. He was pulled to the ground, dragged and kicked.

"Hey, don't kill him! He's worth somethin' alive!"

Ki gritted his teeth against the brutal impact of boots. He fought his way to his feet again, using fists, elbows, teeth, knees, his entire body as a weapon. But it was useless. Despite his spirit, his defiant will, Ki was only human—a human being whose mind and body were exhausted from his brush with the murderous stampede, and drained of their inner force. Blackness overcame him again, and he slumped unconscious to the trail.

His senses returned gradually, as numbed impressions:

The bent-over hunch of his body...

Jarring pain in his wrists, ankles, and belly...

The sight of moonlit ground moving past him at the pace of a horse's walk, and the sound of a complaining voice in back of him...

One other thing Ki knew: he was alive.

He finally became aware of the fact he was tied hand and foot, and that he was jackknifed over a saddle. Craning his head about, he caught sight of two Ryker crewmen, one in front and the other behind him; and of Volpes riding point, mounted on a close-coupled grullo that bore the Snake-Eyes brand on its rump.

"Dunno why the boss picked me to go," the rider in back was whining. "My guts're all busted up inside from that kick, I just know they are, and this jouncin' hurts like pissin' hell."

"Shut up bellerin' like a sick calf," Volpes retorted harshly. "You ain't half as bad off as Mike or Lonnie are, and Fletch here, he can't talk much above a squeak after his throat got squozed."

The riders lapsed into silence, emerging out onto a thin strip of a pass between the mountains and the foothills. They were high, Ki realized, and climbing higher, on a wandering, little-used trail no better than an animal track. More than that, he couldn't tell.

Ki closed his eyes and slumped his head, and quietly tested the ropes binding him. They were tight and well-knotted—but not tight or knotted enough. A slight, humorless smile creased his mouth as he twisted and flexed his wrists and ankles, sensing the weak points. The men, having put their faith in the ropes restraining him, would be less watchful and cautious.

He relaxed then, feeling a bit more confident, and began rebuilding his vital psychic strength. Calming his mind, Ki focused his concentration on an internal point just below his navel, the place the Chinese call *tan t'ien*. As he adjusted his breathing, he continued pressuring the ropes lightly with his wrists and ankles, but he made no overt move to break loose; he was more concerned with restoring his essential energy, and was willing to wait, playing the prisoner, to learn why he was alive. It was no accident; Ki did not believe in luck, but in cause and effect. So there was a reason why he hadn't been killed. To be questioned, he supposed, though he sensed there was more to it than that . . .

For all its meandering, the trail kept generally climbing. In single file, the riders crossed a winding bench and passed through a cloaking pine forest, coming out on the sharp-breaking rim of a narrow canyon. The timber and brush closed down so thickly that the canyon could not have been discovered, even in full daylight, until it was actually entered.

The men veered northward, angling once more over sloping ground until, between two towering rocks, a break in the jagged canyon rim disclosed another ribbony path. As they turned onto it, a guard on the connecting rim came out to the edge, where he could be seen outlined against the soft, starry sky. He did not yell a challenge, but waved questioningly with his arms. Volpes signaled the guard to go on with his job of watching, and they continued along the second trail.

The going was slower now, long night shadows cast by the surrounding mountains blanketing the canyon in darkness. Before he saw the shallow creek, Ki heard Volpes's grullo splashing into the water, followed by the others. They progressed up the stream, its bed widening and deepening as it flowed down around a bend in the now narrowing canyon wall.

Turning the bend himself, Ki glimpsed a point ahead where the two canyon walls apparently joined together to form a land bridge. The water was now up to the withers of the horses, pouring out of what appeared to be the end of a box, over a waterfall some twenty feet in height and about ten wide.

First Volpes and then the next rider disappeared under the falls. Having no choice, Ki moved under the cascading sheet after them, his clothes and aching flesh becoming drenched in the frigid mountain water beating down over him and the horse. On the right, pale moonlight filtered through a narrow passage. They rode into the vague opening, and almost immediately emerged into another, much smaller canyon that was hardly more than a natural pocket dug in the hills.

Not far inside the pocket was a bare-earthed clearing, fronting an elongated log cabin with a flat roof. A few steps from its door were the smoldering embers of a campfire, the silhouettes of three or four men spread out around it. If there were more men in the camp, they were sleeping in the small tarpaper-roofed shacks that dotted the scrub flanking the house; but Ki suspected the shacks were empty, the men out chasing a scattered herd of terrified steers.

116

They rode across the clearing and up before the main cabin. The door opened and a young woman stepped outside, holding a brass night lamp, and looking puffy-eyed and irritated at the men as they dismounted. The two crewmen moved away, out of range of Ki's limited vision. Volpes went up to the girl and said something too low for Ki to hear; and she said something back that was also inaudible, though, judging by the sharpness of its tone, it was probably a rebuke. Ki guessed she was Volpes's girl.

Volpes turned around and walked toward Ki, the girl trailing grudgingly, evidently having been told that her lamp was required. Volpes stopped beside Ki and unsheathed a Green River knife. The girl eased closer, shining the lamp on Ki, her other hand clutching the neck of a long raglan coat, which was draped open around her shoulders, over her nightgown.

Her nightgown was the sort beloved by maiden aunts, of thick daisy-cloth flannel gathered at a yoke in front and back, making it hang very full. But it didn't matter, not on her. Her breasts were plump and high, their large nipples protruding out from the already straining material; and she was leggy down to the warped, mud-caked cowboots that peeked beneath the hem of her gown. Her hair was wrapped in a loose bun at the nape of her neck, and was as raven-black as her eyes, and her butternut-brown face was heart-shaped and matched her body's promise of sensual passion.

One other thing Ki noticed: the girl was Eurasian.

Ki managed a slight nod. *"Yü nü,"* he said.

"Hello yourself." Her black eyes widened, curious, though her mouth remained drawn in a hard, suspicious line.

Volpes had jerked as if bitten. "You've got a fat lip that's gonna get fatter," he snarled, slicing the rope that held Ki down across the saddle.

Ki dropped like a feed sack to the ground, landing on his side. His skull still throbbed and his brains felt as if they were scrambled, from the twin knockouts suffered from the herd and the crewmen. He lay still, breathing through his mouth, as he felt Volpes cut the ropes around his ankles. Then he was hauled to his feet.

"Fletch, goddmam it, c'mere," Volpes yelled, and the man Ki had jabbed in the throat hastened out from the side of the cabin, running bowlegged while he buttoned his fly.

"Put this sassy-assed sonofabitch in the empty shed 'round back," Volpes told him. "And make sure he stays there, 'y'hear?"

Fletch nodded, and pushed Ki ahead of him, causing Ki to stumble slightly, and Ki used the opportunity to glance back and see if the girl was looking his way.

She was, frowning as if perplexed while she stood with Volpes's arm possessively around her waist. Ki grinned. She stiffened, then was hurriedly propelled toward the cabin door, Volpes gripping her tighter and muttering curses.

Ki was pushed forward again, across the yard and along the cabin to the rear, where off to one side stood a small plank-walled shanty with a dark, gaping door. Fletch shoved him inside, and the door slammed shut, and he heard a padlock snapped in heavy chain.

Ki placed his ear against the door. When he could no longer hear Fletch's receding footsteps, he slid down onto the floor and rested his back against the board wall. For a while he merely sat relaxing, and then he began freeing his wrists from the rope.

Focusing all his concentration on the task, Ki purposely dislocated the bones of his wrists, then his hands, even his nimble fingers. Then, by merely twisting and stretching his ligaments and muscles, he slowly wormed his limp, formless flesh through the encoiling bonds. The rope dropped empty to the floor behind his back.

Snapping his bones back into place, Ki swiftly checked his vest pockets. They were all empty, as were his shirt and pants pockets. His daggers were gone, and even his jammed devices holding the *shuriken* were missing. Obviously he'd been searched while he'd been unconscious that second time; and once the men had found the first of his secreted weapons, they must have turned him virtually inside out to locate the rest. He was fortunate to have been left his clothes. Grinning mirthlessly, Ki wondered what they must have thought when they discovered his devices.

He stood, stretching his cramped muscles, and started to cautiously feel around the dark, gloomy shed. He quickly realized that when Volpes had called it empty, he'd been telling the truth.

He settled on the floor again, and fell asleep.

★

Chapter 11

Dawn.

A vague dribble of light began seeping through two thin cracks in the boards across the shed. With a patience he had learned over the years, Ki remained sitting on the same spot where he'd slept, watching the dull gray light ease in time across the flooring. There was no use trying to beat himself against the door and walls, hopelessly wasting his energy. Sooner or later someone had to come in, or he would be led outside. Given a split-second's chance, he would take full advantage of it.

A field mouse scuttled out from a hole and raced around the floor in the feeble light, before returning to its burrow.

Ki thought about that for a while.

Steps sounded outside, and Ki flattened his back to the wall, arms behind him as if the ropes still bound his wrists. The chain rattled slightly, and the padlock made a soft, muffled click. Gently someone pulled the chain loose and eased open the door.

The girl stood outlined against the dawn sky.

"Yü nü," Ki greeted her with a mocking bow of his head. "What, no Volpes?"

"I'm alone. But don't let my nighty fluster you."

"I don't care if you're naked," Ki said. "What I want is in your hands. That is a bowl of soup you're holding, isn't it?"

"Yes," she replied crossly, moving toward him. "And if you don't stop calling me 'fair lady' in that horrid Chinese accent of yours, I'll beat you to death with it. My name is Daphne."

"How fitting," Ki murmured sarcastically.

"Daphne Chung," she continued, "daughter of a coolie spiking track on the Central Pacific, and an Irish camp follower on the Union Pacific. Not that I'd have to kill you, Ki—"

"You know me?"

"I know *of* you. You're all he talked about last night." She squatted in front of Ki and regarded him with her proud onyx eyes. *"He'll* kill you," she said, obviously still meaning Volpes. "Soon's Ryker's finished and turns you over to him, he'll kill you as fast as a trench can be dug. You're dead, Ki, dead."

"Is that why you're here, Daphne? To rub it in?"

"I suppose even a condemned man deserves food," she replied grudgingly, and began spooning soup from the bowl.

Ki kept his arms behind him, getting perverse pleasure out of fooling her. Yet, as she silently helped him eat, another part of his mind was in a quandary, his emotions strangely ambivalent toward this cool-eyed, terse-lipped Eurasian. And when he finished and she asked if that was enough, Ki could only nod dismissively, finding himself unable to thank her for her solicitude.

"That's right, spurn me," she snapped, sensing his rejection. "Daphne the doxy, no better than a second-generation *ukareme.*"

121

Ki gave a sardonic laugh, amused by her use of the antiquated Japanese term for a lewd and dissolute woman. "You're not Japanese," he retorted. "Instead, how about *yü chi?*" Which was equally obsolete Chinese for a third-class "flower girl" who serviced the general public.

She slapped his face, hard, anger flaring in her smoldering black eyes. "Of course, I see now. It's not that I'm a tramp, it's that I'm half Chinese! And the Japanese half of you finds that repugnant, doesn't it? Well, the Japanese make me just as sick."

"Just my luck," Ki sighed. "One of the few times I'm not taken for Chinese, I'm hated for being Jap—"

"Invading us for centuries," she rushed on in her fury, "Ever the conquerer, lording it over us, bloated with superiority and smug contempt!" The girl leaned closer, eyes narrowing, lips peeling back over short, sharp teeth. "But you're the lesser, Ki. At least I'm true to whatever I am. But how false you are to the *yang* of kindness and the *yin* of righteousness, to which you pay lip-service as the basis of your *tsui-kao jih-shih,* your supreme instruction."

Stunned and chagrined by her bitter outburst, Ki could not utter the slightest word of rebuttal. "Daphne, where did you learn . . . ?"

"I was raised by my father, my mother didn't want me. He was a dirt-poor coolie to the West, but to the other Chinese he was a teacher of *T'ai-chi Ch'uan,* the 'supreme ultimate', which makes your pugilism possible—"

She stopped with an abrupt sucking in of air, the sound of heavy footsteps growing louder as they neared the open shed door. Paling, she straightened and backed into one corner, where the shadows were deepest, lines of fear suddenly creasing her almond-hued face.

"Hell, looky there," a man's voice growled. "The door ain't locked like it orter be. Guess this's my lucky day."

A weasel-faced man strutted bowlegged into the shed, and stood with legs apart, fists resting cockily on his hips. "Well, now, I heard tell you was here," he said to Ki, walking closer, and then his sneering grin widened when he glimpsed Daphne hunching in the corner. "Didn't know you was here too, gal. Guess none of us did, 'specially Volpes. Maybe we can fix it so he don't find out, eh?"

Snickering, he turned back to Ki. "Know who I is?"

"Not by name," Ki said with a slight quiver to his voice, hoping to draw the man out. "Didn't I see you the other night in the saloon?"

"Right, boy. You saw me there, gettin' my hide blistered by that uppity galfriend of yours. Seems she ain't the only bitch liking yaller meat, is she?" the man added, leering at Daphne again.

"I'll tell him," Daphne hissed. "I swear I will."

"You ain't tellin' Volpes nothin'," the man retorted snidely. "You ain't got the guts to. Ain't got much brains, either. If'n you're gonna fool around on him, you orter leastwise have the sense to do it on the sly. Keep it private, like this." He pulled the door shut, plunging the shed into murky dimness, and returned to Ki, nudging him with the toe of his boot. "Ryker's sendin' a note to your gal, boy, tellin' her he's got you hid, an' if'n she wants you back, she'd better come collect you. You're bait, boy, live bait. 'Cept I've gotta a few scores to square on my own, an' the way I sees it, I got the chance, and nobody's told me how 'live you've gotta be."

"Leave him alone, Nealon, and get the hell out!"

"I'll tend to you in a minute, slut," Lloyd Nealon snarled, and rearing, he kicked Ki viciously in the stomach.

Ki, anticipating, had already used an exercise to relax his muscles, and the kick hurt hardly at all. Straightening from his sitting position, arms still behind him, he said coldly, "Try that again, and I'll kill you."

The former Flying W foreman laughed derisively. "Why, you nervy asshole, I'm gonna give you a taste of whupping, like I whupped ol' man Waldemar." Drawing his sixgun, Nealon swung a pistol-whipping blow with his right hand while gut-punching with his left, adding, "Only this ain't gonna look like no accident!"

Ki killed him.

Ducking, Ki gripped the revolver and bent it back, breaking Nealon's trigger finger with a spasmodic firing of one shot. Ignoring the bullet slamming upwards into the low roof, and the explosion thundering in the tiny shed, Ki firmed the hold of his other hand on the arm of the first aiming for his stomach. In a blur of motion, Ki spun Nealon with *kuwatago*—a short "flying mare" toss that sent Nealon sailing over his shoulder.

Nealon landed on his back, screaming as his pelvis cracked. Then he stopped screaming as Ki kicked in the side of his head, crushing the temple bone like an eggshell.

"I'll dump the garbage," Ki said affably, glancing at Daphne. She was standing rigid in the corner, face flushed, mouth wide, and it seemed to Ki that a faint gleam of hope lit her eyes. He wasn't sure; perhaps he imagined it, he thought as he lifted Nealon, but it seemed that way to him.

He dragged Nealon by the collar and belt, using the man's broken skull to push open the door. With a swing, he heaved the corpse outside, where it landed, mucous and blood spewing from its mouth and nose, just as seven men came rushing up, pistols in hand.

The man in the lead was yelling, "The shot came from—" Then, seeing the body and Ki standing in the doorway, they pulled up short. "Look what he done to Lloyd! Gun him!"

"Go ahead," Ki called, smiling. "Shoot."

Seven revolvers were leveled, fingers squeezing triggers.

"Shoot me," Ki urged again. "Ryker will love you for it."

The men hesitated, frustrated by uncertainty.

Shrugging, Ki stepped back inside and calmly closed the door.

Daphne came toward him, her voice a whisper. "You are a *lei jen*, a man of thunder . . ." Her words were momentarily lost in the noise of the men running up outside and rechaining the door. She went ashen, hearing the snap of the padlock, and when she spoke again, her voice was no longer hushed. It was hard, loud, and angry. "You're also a fool! Why didn't you just keep going while you were out there?"

"I wasn't finished."

"You're finished!" she said furiously. "Oh, God, you are!"

"A man of thunder? What difference if I'm made of thunder or not?" Ki snapped back. "I'm still a man, and a man can't get far with seven revolvers aiming point-blank at him."

"We're both finished," Daphne moaned, slumping to the floor. "We're both locked in here now. We're trapped!"

★

Chapter 12

Jessica continued her dogged search, going over the same ground again and again, trying to spot fresh details each time. But Ki was gone, vanished, most likely dead. As long as he had been with her, his optimism and courage had sustained her. Now, without him, Jessica felt at her heart the cold hand of futility and grief.

Yet she refused to admit her fears, to accept the obvious. Some small doubt wormed in her mind, and its persistent squirmings sharpened her eyes. Bloodstains. In a wide patch near the boulders across from Ki's dead horse, she glimpsed splattered blood like freckles, and wondered how she'd missed them all the times before.

She stood back a short distance to survey their pattern, curious about how these stains looked different from the smudges and pools around the dead steers, horses, and rustlers. It almost looked as if it had been caused not by the stampede, but by a fight, a scuffle of some sort.

Moving into the area, Jessica hunkered down and began to study it inch by inch, trying to sort out and piece together what had happened here. She found bootprints, a lot of them, pivoting and squirreling in all directions, as if following the call of some odd, macabre dance. Then her practiced eye caught the faint, scuffed outline of Ki's distinctive rope-soled slippers.

Pulse quickening, she hunted for more. She found a few, a very few, but was able to make out where Ki had evidently been dragged to where six or seven horses had stood. All the hoof-prints that left the area were pointing toward the plateau. One of the horses, she saw, had a cracked fore shoe.

Swiftly she returned to her horse and rode out of the gorge. Reaching the mouth of the canyon, where the herd had spread out across the plateau, she dismounted and started another painstaking search for some sign of that broken shoe. Locating it, she swung back into her saddle and followed it across the plateau to the entrance of the pass leading to the Block-Two-Dot.

There the horse had stopped with the others for a long enough while to leave droppings and splashes of urine. Scouting, Jessica determined that the bunch was definitely seven in number, joined by an eighth horse coming up out of the pass. She felt a sneaky hunch that the eighth had been ridden by Ryker, after she'd found the butt of an expensive Havana cigar doused in one of the urine puddles.

The meeting had split up, with four of the horses going into the pass. The other four, including the horse with the broken shoe, had angled westward toward the rising slopes of the mountains beyond.

Jessica trailed the broken shoe. It was easily traced across the plateau, but once it entered the rocky, forested uplands, the going got more difficult.

Jessica took her time, gauging the vast raw stone and wooded scrub for the dim, indistinct clues of passage. Much of her tracking was done by instinct; once she went a half-mile up a culvert free of any sign at all before she found that her trust had been good. A white scratch, the iron of a horseshoe against a rock...and then, a little farther on, a stepped-on twig, cracked and showing pulp.

The path kept close to the contours of the foothills, rarely along the ridges, but through clefts and hollows. Most of it seemed little used, and at that, mostly by game.

Once, when she discovered a solid imprint of a hoof, she stopped and examined it closely. The edges hadn't crumbled, but there were indications of dew; the track had been made early last night. She continued on with grim satisfaction. Twice more she had to rein in and study the terrain, unraveling the path as it wove higher among the crags and spurs and overgrown canyons.

The creek brought her to another halt. It was a fast-rippling flow cutting right across the trail—but it quickly became apparent that the tracks didn't come out the other side. They entered at an upstream angle and stayed in the water. Turning, Jessica headed up along the creek, riding slowly while scrutinizing both banks for wet impressions of the horses having left the creekbed.

The canyon slopes rose higher and drew nearer, becoming cliffs hemming her into a narrow culvert. The only tracks she found were those of animals that had come to drink. By now it was well into midmorning, the day proving to be overcast, the air cool and very still. Too still. The lack of noise bothered Jessica, for if the rocks ahead were devoid of humans, she should have been able to hear little scuttlings, tiny chirps and buzzings.

She moved on, increasingly wary of her surroundings.

The creek grew wider and deeper, making an S-curve, a swath of tall grasses and a few saplings sprouting in its bend. Rounding it, Jessica saw that the creek rushed disjointedly from between boulders, down from a collecting pond and a short waterfall. Slowly she continued parallelling the creek on a moss-covered ledge, a cold clammy sensation nestling between her shoulder blades.

A gravelly voice said, "Hold it, sister, and get down."

Jessica reined sharply and dismounted, seeing a thickset man with stubbly cheeks and watery eyes emerge from the rocks just ahead. The Winchester he pointed was all the more dangerous for his shaky trigger finger.

"Been spyin' you since you came into the pass," the man said, coming closer, eyeballing her and licking lips like slices of liver. "What's your name, sister, and whatcha doing way up here?"

"Imogene," Jessica said demurely.

"Yeah? Imogene what?"

"Just . . . Imogene. I find last names kind of get in the way between friends, don't you?"

The man laughed once, derisively. "What're you doing here?"

"Well, I was out riding, and I got ever so lost."

"Balls."

"Truth, mister. If you could direct me back to—"

"Nobody can get so damned lost that they wind up back in this buzzard's roost, and you know it. Now, why're you really here?"

Jessica smiled shyly and folded her hands in front of her, thumbs hooking behind her belt buckle. "I reckon I can't fool a big smart man like you. I'm looking for the rustlers."

"The—? What'n hell you want us—them—for?"

"You got to understand, mister, I'm new to Eucher Butte, having run out of luck down Cheyenne way. But the dance places, like the Thundermug, are all full up and don't need new talent, and I'm kind of broke, and a girl has to make a living, y'know what I mean?"

The man's face remained poker straight. "No, tell me."

"Well, when I heard about a bunch of men hid out up in these hills, it seemed to me that if they couldn't come to me, I'd go to them. So, if by some chance you could help me—if you could escort me to their camp, I'd be grateful. *Very* grateful."

"I ain't that crazy! Once you got in there with all them, I wouldn't get nothing for a month of Sundays." The man backed a pace, raising his rifle and gesturing with it. "Get into the bushes, Imogene, I'm taking you all for myself."

The bullet entered his stomach while he was still gesturing with his rifle. It hit low, straight, shot from Jessica's derringer when she snapped the hidden pistol out from behind her belt buckle. The man seemed paralyzed from the impact of the .38 slug, mouth wide as if to scream, but no sound coming out.

Jessica was in motion even as the bullet struck. She leaped for the man, snatching the rifle from his nerveless fingers and springing for the cover of the nearby rocks. She crouched, waiting.

The man stayed upright, although his knees were gradually bending. He clasped both hands against the wound, trying to hold himself together, his rolling eyes glazed and disbelieving as he stared down at his red-staining shirtfront. His legs buckled; he toppled over, slowly crumpling to sprawl inert.

Jessica stayed put, drawing her revolver, then reloading the derringer and slipping it back behind her buckle. Her horse browsed near the stream, shaking its head once. The man lay absolutely still, his hands pressed to his midriff, his face retaining its startled expression, as if sealed by wax. Jessica ignored them both, her attention centering on the crevices and shadowed nooks above and around them.

She had killed again. To keep from being raped, true, although she'd purposely tricked the man into believing she was a whore. And if he'd agreed to take her to the rustlers' hideout—where, she was convinced, the tracks she was following ultimately led—she wouldn't have shot him. At least not right then, and maybe later it wouldn't have been necessary. But she had only a moment to spare for remorse; there was a job that needed to be done.

By the time flies had begun to gather on the man, Jessica was pretty sure no partner was hiding, anticipating revenge. Nonetheless, she took care. She dashed from the rocks and grabbed the man's legs, then hustled them both behind cover. After another long pause, she darted out again and led her horse into the rocks, where, out of sight of the brook, she tied its reins to a tree.

Alive, the man had virtually admitted being one of the rustlers; dead, he told her two other important facts: he must have been posted as a sentry, and he hadn't gotten wet on the job or while stalking her. Which meant, Jessica figured, that the hideout had to be nearby, on this side of the stream. On the surface, that didn't add up too well, because obviously neither the rustlers nor the horses she'd been tracking were anywhere in the canyon, and the waterfall ahead was pouring over what was essentially the canyon's rear wall. Yet she felt her hunch was right when she glimpsed a pale drift of smoke rising from the hills beyond; it was scarcely more than a thin, indistinguishable smudge against the drab skyline, but it was enough to confirm that somewhere up there to her left, somebody was using green wood to fuel a campfire.

From here, she would go on foot.

★

Chapter 13

Tempering her impatience, Jessica scouted the area, then cautiously started up the slope of the canyon. She climbed at a crawl as the morning eased toward noon with a light sprinkling of rain. There was a tenseness to the cooling drizzle, a hush as if the hills resented her and the thickening slurry of clouds, and it made Jessica watchful and slightly nervous. Nearing the rim, she groped for handholds in the weathered rock, testing each one before placing her weight on it; the cracked, fissured stone crumbled easily in her fingers. Once she almost lost her balance and toppled back into the chasm of the stream. She clawed frantically, pressing against the cliff face and grabbing onto an outcropping that trembled and fell loose as she hauled herself to another high point.

Easing over the top, she flattened herself, trying to catch her breath from the last desperate pull. For long moments the pounding blood in her ears made her deaf to the gravel and dirt trickling down the way she'd come. Then she started forward, keeping low and in line with the upper course of the stream, as it bubbled and stewed toward the surging waterfall on her right.

She entered a tangle of shrubs and stunted trees, whose windswept limbs were twisted at every conceivable angle. She stood in their shadows a while, silently listening for men and looking for that telltale ribbon of smoke. Then, moving to her left, away from the waterfall, she struggled through a cluttered grove of conifers, eventually emerging where a rotted tree had settled, roots upended, by the very edge of a straight-sided drop.

Crouching on the ledge and concealed by a low hedge of brush, Jessica peered over the side into a small, box-shaped pocket canyon. It was slightly at an angle to the other canyon, a land-bridge connecting the two; and either through erosion or upheaval, the bed of the stream skirted the pocket and formed the waterfall at the narrowest point of the land-bridge. A curious quirk of nature, but not uncommon; mountains were like this, concealing deep pockets till one stood on their very brink.

Most of the pocket was overgrown with tall grass, scrub, and thickets of aspen, fir, and pine. But a quarter of the way in from the land-bridge, at a tangent to the waterfall, she saw a log cabin and some motley shacks clustered around a wide clearing, in the middle of which burned the fire whose smoke she'd spotted. A path led from the clearing to a point below and just to one side of the waterfall—the pocket's only entrance, Jessica assumed, though she couldn't make it out precisely because of her distance and poor angle.

Four men were standing at the fire, cooking something in a cast-iron kettle. Another fourteen or fifteen men could be seen elsewhere in and about the clearing, walking, talking, or doing nothing, ignoring their scattered equipment and the loose cavvy of untended saddle horses. Obviously the men were lazy, badly organized, and poorly disciplined, which didn't surprise Jessica; and whatever else they were, they were not defense-conscious. The chain of tall ridges surrounding the pocket, watched over by the now-dead guard, was evidently trusted to be protection enough; a single shot would warn them, and they were camped in a natural fort, a hole-in-the-wall that had one hidden gap through which they could be attacked.

Since it was impossible from here to detect which, if any, of the horses wore a broken shoe, Jessica ignored the cavvy and concentrated on the men. She searched out each one to see if she could recognize any. They were depressingly similar, dressed in grubby shirts and pants, needing shaves and trims, none with a three-fingered hand, say, or only one ear. No peculiarities at all. No Ryker, no Volpes, and most discouragingly, no Ki.

Jessica sat back, contemplating. If Ki was in the pocket, he was either imprisoned or buried. Of course, she had no way of knowing if he was down there; she'd been following horses, not men. Back when the eight horses had split up at that pass, she'd chosen the broken-shoe trail because the other trail appeared to simply head to the Block-Two-Dot. For her to brave Ryker's stronghold alone would have been foolhardy; to have gone there first, and not found Ki, would have also allowed time and weather to obliterate the meager traces and signs leading to the canyon. But whether Ki was down there or back at Ryker's, there was no doubt in her mind about the men she could see. Trash. Nor did she question *if* she should do something about them, only *what* she should do about them. Afterwards, she'd allow herself the luxury of feeling regret. But only afterwards.

Jessica thought a bit longer, then slipped back into the brush and began hiking back to the bluff overlooking the canyon. She took her time, not risking detection, yet she wanted to hurry, knowing that sooner or later someone would be detailed to relieve the dead sentry. Reaching the spot where she'd climbed up, she started her treacherous way back down again, sliding and plunging, digging in her heels and clutching with her hands to keep from tripping into a headlong dive.

Once at the bottom of the creek, she hurried to remount her horse and ride back out of the canyon, still keeping a cautious eye on the terrain around her. Without lingering, she entered the maze of crooked ridges and twisting gorges, hoping her sense of direction would not fail her, scouting steadily through the roughs of brush, rock, and forests for familiar marks that would lead her back to the plateau. Twice she followed false sign and had to backtrack, the wasted time frustrating her, making her edgy. If she was a good enough tracker to find the canyon, she chastised herself, then at least she ought to be able to track her own goddamn backtrail out again.

Finally she reined in and smiled, seeing the plateau up ahead. She headed out across it, toward the mouth of the canyon from which the rustled cattle had fled, figuring to pick up the path there that would return her to the Spraddled M. Approaching, she saw that the last leg of her trip was unnecessary. Daryl Melville was standing just inside the canyon mouth, holding the reins of his buckskin. Beside him, Deputy Oakes had one foot on the ground and the other lodged in his stirrup, in the process of either getting on or off a moro with tan leggings. Spotting her, Daryl began gesturing and moving forward to meet her, while the deputy merely put his stirruped foot down and waited.

"God, but I was worried about you," Daryl called, even before she could come to a halt and dismount. "When I woke and you weren't—I mean, I guessed you'd come here to look for your friend, but then when I couldn't find you . . . you should've told me, Jessica!"

"Oh, it wasn't that important," she said vaguely, smiling as if the whole thing had been just a whim of hers. "Certainly not so important that you should've called the law in."

"He didn't, ma'am," the deputy said, answering for Daryl as he politely removed his hat. "No, ma'am, I was over looking for you at the hotel, and they said you might've gone to the Flying W, so I rode there and they said you might've gone visiting the Spraddled M. Then I got tooken here. My, you sure do lead a feller a merry chase."

"He don't believe what happened," Daryl said grimly.

"Now, Daryl, you're givin' Miss Starbuck the wrong impression," Deputy Oakes replied gruffly. "I ain't deputin' that a wad of steers broke crazy down that gorge, or that a few Block-Two-Dot punchers were trompled. I'm only queryin' the drift you've put on it, is all. Seems to me it's as liable that the men were trying to head off them rustlers behind the cows, or coming in to help you."

"They were after us, I tell you, aiming to kill us!"

"Well, if they caught you trespassin', like you admit, I can't rightly blame them if some tempers got a little het up and—"

"Deputy," Jessica cut in sharply, "why're you looking for me?"

"Oh, yes, that," Oakes said with a haggard sigh. "What with this here in the gorge and everythin', the day's been kinda discombobulatin'." He reached into his hat and brought out a rumpled, slightly sweat-stained envelope. "Here, this is addressed to you."

The envelope had no marks or postage on it, only her name and the words URGENT, DELIVER IMMEDIATELY written on its front, and what appeared to be a knife-slice through its middle. Jessica ripped it open and removed a sheet of onionskin, also cut, and read:

Dear Miss Starbuck:

I believe you're missing an item of sentimental importance. If you wish to arrange a recovery, you know where to contact me. I urge you to do so promptly, to assure undamaged condition, and I also insist that as proof of your goodwill, you come alone.

Guthried Ryker

"Horseshit," Jessica murmured under her breath, then louder, to Deputy Oakes, she snapped, "Where'd you get this?"

"The workmen found it stuck with a knife to my office

door, when they went there this morning to rebuild the cells. Gawd, what a mess." Oakes nervously clutched his hatbrim in both hands. "Can't add more'n that, ma'am. It's all I know."

Jessica refolded the note and stuck it back into the envelope, saying to Daryl, "Ryker's got Ki. He wants me to go to the ranch."

"The bastard! You can't, Jessica, it's a trap."

"Sure it is," Jessica agreed, nodding. "I know it, and Ryker knows I know it, but he's counting on my coming anyway. I don't have any choice, he thinks, because I don't have any idea where he's got Ki hidden. I'm forced to play his game his way. But Ki isn't at Ryker's place. Ryker's too shrewd to risk a charge of kidnapping. He made sure not to write anything incriminating in his note, but he wouldn't have sent it at all, if he had Ki where he could be found at the ranch. Though that's what he'd like me to believe." Jessica paused, eyes narrowing, a tight, flinty smile creasing her lips. "But what Ryker doesn't know is that I *do* know where Ki is."

Swiftly she sketched the events since she'd discovered the blood-spattered scene of the struggle in the gorge, as the two men listened with mouths gaping in surprise. She told of tracking the broken-shoed horse to the canyon, and described the natural pocket in which she'd located the camp, while Daryl breathed harshly with increasing anger, and Deputy Oakes grew redder in his fat jowls.

"So," Jessica concluded, "Ryker's note has backfired on him. He's unwittingly answered which of the two places Ki must've been taken."

"Him and his filthy kidnappers!" Daryl roared furiously. "God knows how long he's had them nesting up there, swooping down like vultures to steal our stock and now people! There you are, Oakes!"

"There I am, what?"

"She's found our rustlers. What're you going to do about 'em?"

"I, uh...I suppose a posse, and, uh..." The deputy

hesitated, scratching his hair, and then he clapped his hat back on, a crafty glint coming to his eyes. "Hold on, won't do to go off half cocked. I gotta investigate this first, legal and proper. Now, Miss Starbuck, did I hear you admit that this here letter you got don't exactly spell out a kidnapping or ransom demand?"

"No, but it's implied, and Ki was taken by Ryker's men."

"Your friend may be missing, ma'am, but did you actually see him being taken, or being held against his will in that camp? And these here kidnappers—can you prove they're Block-Two-Dot men, and if so, that they're following Mr. Ryker's orders? Or that they're the rustlers, who you figure are also working for Mr. Ryker?"

Jessica glared at Oakes.

"No?" he said. "Well, ma'am, I need evidence 'fore I can organize a posse and go rousting innercent folk. I mean, d'you have proof the men in the camp are the rustlers? Did you see any stolen cattle with 'em?"

"Of course not. That pocket's too small for much more than their camp," Jessica replied frostily. "But I've got a strong hunch, Deputy, that maybe you can tell us where those cows are."

"Me? Not me," Oakes retorted indignantly. "I haven't any idea who the rustlers are, or what they've done with the stock."

"You should. It's part of your job, only Ryker's paid you to be blind to it, hasn't he? That's why you could never trace them."

"Lady, you're loco," Oakes growled, but his voice was quivering. Sensing that his denials were getting him nowhere, he again tried to attack: "Fact is, I'm thinkin' you're trying to trick me! You're trying to ruin me and disgrace Mr. Ryker, our most prominent citizen, so you can go ahead with your own dirty work!"

"Stop blustering," Daryl raged. "You're caught."

"Nope *you're* caught, both of you!" Oakes stepped closer to Daryl, his pudgy hand groping in his hip pocket for his handcuffs. "For trespassin', disturbin' the peace, bearin' false witness, and suspicion of havin' a hand in stampedin' them cows—"

Daryl's fist whipped out in a short, pistonlike punch that connected with the deputy's chin. Oakes's head whipped back and he crumpled to the rain-dampened earth, blood oozing from his mouth.

Jessica stooped and snatched his revolver from its holster, while Daryl rolled him over and snapped the cuffs on his wrists.

"There are some spare piggin' strings in my saddlebags," Daryl said, as he wrestled to lift the mud-splotched deputy onto his horse. "See if you can use them to tie his legs to the stirrups."

Fetching the strings, Jessica asked, "He's coming along?"

"Yeah, to make some arrests, even if he's in no mind to."

Oakes, regaining his wits while he slumped in his saddle, glowered and cursed them, swearing to have them both in jail by nightfall. His moro didn't seem to appreciate his language, and started prancing, its tan leggings flashing droplets of the continuing drizzle. Oakes promptly shut up, straining to keep his seat.

"I hope you fall on that fat head of yours," Daryl told him, then turned to Jessica. "Now let's get to gathering all the hands from my ranch and the Flying W, and then we'll go rescue your friend."

Jessica, startled, restrained him with her hand. "Please, Daryl, I appreciate your offer, but I can't have all of you risk—"

"Don't you argue, Jessie," he fumed. "I thought we had this all sorted out last night. You may've come here to make this your fight, and Ki may be the reason you're fighting now. Hell, I like the feller too. But this was *our* fight first, and it goes a lot deeper than just one man—or woman. And by God, I aim to see it finished."

Jessica nodded and smiled. "All right, offer accepted."

"Y'think we should get the other ranchers in on it?"

"Frankly, I don't. If you're determined to do this, then

it'll take too much time to reach them, explain, and get their crews together. Besides, we'll have enough men to surround the rim of the pocket and cover the entrance hole. The rustlers don't realize it, but if we can hold them down in there, they're virtually sitting ducks."

Daryl mulled it over for a moment, then said with a frown, "Listen, I'd better warn you, and if you don't like it, you'd better say no. Way I see it, it's going to be a fight to the death, no quarter given. If we bottle them up like you say, and knock them all to hell an' gone, Ki is liable to get hurt permanent-like."

"Daryl, Ki is either already dead—and as you told me last night, dead's dead—or he's being kept locked in someplace. And if that's the case, what we've got to do is attack so swiftly and surprisingly that the rustlers won't have a chance to bring him out and use him as a hostage. They'll be too busy fighting us."

"Well, I still figure his odds stink."

"Maybe so, Daryl, but they're worse every other way. If we tried to simply ram through the pocket's entrance, we'd suffer awful losses, and never reach Ki in time. If we do nothing, eventually he'll be killed anyway, and if I do what Ryker's note demands, it'll only result in my dying with him. I know Ki; given a sliver of a chance, he can take care of himself better than any man alive. And I also know that this is the way Ki would want it."

But she was equally aware that Daryl was right—this was a frightful risk to take. If Ki wasn't gunned by the rustlers in retaliation or panic, he could just as easily be caught in the murderous crossfire that the two crews would be pouring down into the pocket. That is, if Ki was still alive—if Ryker's cutthroat gang hadn't already slaughtered him out of sheer cussedness.

★
Chapter 14

Ki was very much alive.

And he was feeling more alive with each passing moment. He was in trouble, but it was trouble he'd been figuring might be turned to his own disadvantage. Daphne Chung was spoiling his chances of that. Just the mere presence of Volpes's willful, mischievous lover was adding a potentially volatile threat he couldn't predict and guard against. Yet he couldn't look on her barely clothed, provocative sultriness and miss the feeling that here was a devastating female whose survival ability was centered between her legs. Her fiery challenge was unspoken, an undercurrent he was determined to defend himself against.

Not that he didn't want her.

That was the problem. He did.

She was staring up at him from where she was slumped beside him on the dirty shed floor. The frightened sheen was dimming from her eyes, and she was watching him with, it seemed to Ki, something like fascination. He expected her to continue tongue-lashing him. He waited, but no more furious outbursts came.

Finally he said, "Stop sulking. If anybody's trapped in here, it's me, not you." He said it harshly—too harshly, as if directing some of it inward—and instantly relented. "Hell, Daphne, you've got nothing to worry about. When the door opens, you can explain."

"No, he'll kill me. He owns me."

"Volpes just wants to scare you into thinking he does."

"He owns me, Ki. And he's warned me that if he ever catches me with another man, he'll kill me. He means it, he will."

"A bowl of soup isn't very compromising."

"In my gown, without getting his permission first, it is. Oh, he'll know the soup was only an excuse, he'll know what I was after."

"Mind letting me know?"

"I was going to make you promise that if I . . . if I released you, helped you escape, you'd take me with you."

Ki raked her face with a quick, questioning look, and saw that her gaze was intent and pleading. "You vixen, you really were."

"I certainly was." Her voice was low and husky with emotion, and made Ki feel warm inside. She caught his arm and tugged him down to sit with her, then leaned over and pressed her lips against his mouth. When he started wrapping his arms around her, she pushed away. "There, you see? Any way I had to, I was."

Ki felt her warm breath against his face and smelled her womanly fragrance, and read in her anguished gaze the strength of a soul living with a truth that is against it. "Oh, yes, Ki, I'm a passionate girl. I take lots of loving. But you know, all I've ever really wanted was to be liked. I've been pushed down, sat down, thrown down, and upside-downed, but never turned down. Never simply liked for myself. Who could, considering what I am?"

"Don't hate yourself, Daphne. I don't."

"You do, you don't have to lie. It's too late now, but the worst part is that I'd been waiting for you a long, long while."

Again, Ki studied her eyes for meaning, and this time she smiled. "That's a silly thing for me to say, isn't it?" she murmured. "When I couldn't have been waiting for you, since I didn't know you existed till late last night."

"It could do with some explaining, yes."

"It's not a pretty story." Her voice was unsteady. "Volpes bought my contract from a house in Salinas. Utah, that is, not Kansas. It cost him a bundle. I was the . . . resident virgin, and virgins can make a house a fortune. Anyway, he's always led a gang, long as I've known him. His men change, but it's always the same—thieving, rustling, robbing trains—and he's kept me with him in a dozen different hideouts, getting his money's worth, you could say."

Daphne was clinging gently to Ki's midriff as she confessed her torment, her fingers circling of their own volition. Ki felt a prurient stirring in his loins, triggered by her longing, and sparked by a perverse physical yearning that was building between them. He tried to resist. Another time, another place, he'd have flattened her to the nearest bed without hesitation, but here?

"Okay, I get the picture," Ki said curtly, feeling himself hardening against his will. He tried to shift where he sat, his beginning erection bulging out the crotch of his pants. "So you don't like it, you're fed up with him. Fine. So leave him."

"I have, quite a few times. He always brings me back and beats me, beats me so hard he's broken my bones before. Now that Ryker's hired him and his gang, and installed them up here, there's no way I can get free without . . ." There was a sob in her voice now. "I could only wait, Ki. Wait for a strong man I could trust."

"For a crazy man willing to die for you, you mean."

"No, no!" she replied in a thick whisper, and on her face was a look of sudden excitement. "To live for me, Ki, not die! Haven't you ever felt that about a girl, Ki?"

Ki didn't answer.

"Not ever?"

"Never mind." He glanced away from her searching eyes, from her lips and breasts and legs, her nightgown hiked up almost to her thighs from the awkward way she was sitting.

"Ki?"

"Yes?"

"I don't know if I love you, but I want you."

"Stop it."

"I've wanted you since the second I laid eyes on you. I want you now, right now, in spite of everything. *Because* of everything."

"You don't want me, Daphne. You're just upset."

"I do . . . and you want me. You're hard, hard as a bar of iron. I can feel you poking my arm, Ki." She giggled lightly, and languidly began to strip off her nightgown. Unbuttoning it at the throat, she crossed her arms and with slow, tantalizing suggestiveness, eased the gown up over her head and tossed it aside. "There. Now you."

For a moment Ki did not move, could not move, his eyes feasting on her nudity. Her breasts, golden and firm, nipples large and jutting like ripe black cherries. Her belly, taut and flat, flaring down into rich black curls of pubic hair, the pink flesh of her vaginal lips peeking warmly from underneath. Her thighs, smooth and tapering into long legs that he instinctively knew would wrap around him in a squeezing grip of passion.

Then, goaded to recklessness, Ki removed vest and shirt, and rose to unbuckle his pants, aroused, throbbingly erect, aching to penetrate her voluptuous body. Her hands reached high, her fingers burning his flesh as she began pulling his pants down, her gaze riveted on his naked loins, her breath coming in short, hissing gasps. Daphne was in heat, animal heat, and Ki knew there was no longer any denying her—or himself.

His left trouser leg off, he balanced on his left foot while they both tore at his right trouser leg. Daphne, gazing hurgrily at his jutting instrument, giggled again. "Position eighty, *Chin Chi Tu Li*."

"What?" Then Ki got it. "Oh, yes, your father's *T'ai-chi* exercises—'Golden Cock Stands On One Leg'."

He settled alongside her, moving one hand down over the smoothness of her buttocks, marveling in their warm texture and beautiful shape. She tilted her face and kissed him urgently, her hand searching down between them and closing around his burgeoning shaft. He sucked in his breath, his blood pounding as she stroked him with her fingertips and nails, and then he crushed the full length of her body against his, grinding his pelvis into her.

"Yes, now," she moaned. "Now, I beg you . . ."

Ki pulled her beneath him, and she opened her legs to accept his thrust between them. He could feel her crevice moist and tender against the blunt crown of his erection, and thinking to repay her, he taunted, "Position sixty-three, *Yeh Ma Fên Tsung*—'Partition of Wild Horse's Mane,'" as he slid gently through her pubic hair.

"And *Shê Shen Hsia Shih*," she moaned, "'The Snake Creeps Down,'" feeling Ki plunge fully into her loins, her hips slowly undulating against him. Her thighs pressed against his legs as her ankles wrapped over and locked around his calves. He pumped deep into her soft flesh while she strained under him, moaning beneath his rhythmic surges, opening and closing her thighs, her head thrashing from side to side on the cold shed floor with total abandon. *"K'ua Hu! K'ua Hu!"* she chanted. "'Ride The Tiger'!"

Ki could feel himself growing and expanding inside her till he felt as if he were going to explode from the exquisite pleasure building in his groin, and he could sense that Daphne was also nearing completion as she gripped him tighter and moved more frantically under him, reveling in his thrusts, hot and pulsating and deep.

"Now, Ki, now! *Pao Hu Kwei Shan!* 'Carry the Tiger to the Mountain'!" she pleaded, urging him on with the pounding of her heels on his legs. Then she cried out shrilly, loud and piercing, uncaring if it brought the camp running.

145

Ki didn't give a damn either, ejaculating violently into her as she shuddered convulsively beneath him with each of his pulsing spurts.

Then Daphne's body collapsed limply and she was still, except for the uncontrollable quivering of her thighs still firmly pressed around his loins. And Ki remained inside her, feeling himself drained of energy, placidly satiated.

"Forgive me . . . forgive me . . ." Daphne murmured crushing her lips against his mouth before he could respond, then pulling away as abruptly as she'd clung. "You must think terribly of me, Ki, and I don't blame you. But, oh, I wanted you . . . needed you . . . I still do . . ."

A shaft of waning sunlight filtered through a crack in the wall, illuminating her face under him, and revealing a smile that was sad, and yet warm and tender. Ki wanted to tell her now that he didn't think less of her, only of himself for having given in to the risk of being caught like this. And to tell the truth, he didn't even care much about that. Their coupling somehow seemed natural, even though the circumstances were unnatural; their joining had served to release their dangerously pent-up emotions.

But Ki was a fighter, not a poet. He found it impossible to voice what he only dimly perceived in his instinctive reaction to her sensuality. He drew her to him instead, answering her fears in his own way, by hungrily kissing the smoothness of her lips, her neck, the swelling nipples of her breasts.

"Ki . . . Ki . . ." Daphne cried, while her naked flesh began to tingle with renewed excitement. Tears blurred her eyes, and her voice was thick with desire and fright. "Don't leave me, don't . . ."

"I won't," he assured her as he tongued one nipple.

"Take me with you. Please, take me away from here."

"If I can."

"And don't die for me, Ki, live for me . . ."

"I'll keep living . . . living as I am now."

And he was alive, he had to admit wryly. He could feel himself harden within her, swelling into stiff, reinvigorated

146

passion. He tentatively thrust deeper into her.

Daphne gasped with delight. "You can't . . . !"

"I am," Ki chuckled throatily. *"Hai Ti Chên."*

"'Needle at Sea Bottom,' it is indeed," she sighed, arching and writhing underneath him—then she suddenly screamed, freezing rigid.

Ki twisted his head sideways to see what had shocked her into mortal terror. And he just kept on twisting, withdrawing from Daphne and swiveling around in an upright crouch, readying to strike.

The shed door was open. Not by very much, but enough to admit Volpes. "I thought I heard that squawk of yours," he snarled at Daphne, stepping closer as she scuttled into an almost fetal position. "So I was real quiet about unlocking and sliding the chain loose, and I'm glad I was. But shit! I could've fired a cannon off in here and not disturbed you, the way you were bucking and snorting!"

"I—I'm sorry," she whined. "I'll never do—"

"You're right, you won't." Volpes loomed menacingly over her; and Ki, who'd been cursing himself for being as blindly preoccupied as Daphne, made a motion to stop Volpes from touching the girl. Volpes, pivoting and drawing his pistol, yelled out, "Boys!"

The door swung wider and three more men rushed in, grinning rapaciously and bristling with revolvers. Ki tensed to take them on too, but then thought better of it; Volpes now had his pistol aimed at Daphne, and he looked ready to shoot her at the slightest provocation.

"No, I wasn't ignoring you," Volpes told Ki with a sideways glare. "I was saving you. Killed one of my men, I hear. Just bashed his head in. And now you've been dipping your wick in my woman. You've got brass balls, boy." He glanced at his men then, ordering, "This chink so much as breathes, blow those balls off."

There was a chorus of lewd snickers, while the girl huddled naked and cringing.

Volpes, concentrating on Daphne again, shouted, "Get up, you slut!" And when she didn't, he holstered his revolver

147

and wrapped his hand in her hair, whipping her upright. "You fuckin' li'l whore!" With his other hand, he smashed a brutal fist to her jaw, and she sagged limply, still held standing by her hair.

Volpes dragged her to the nearest two men. "Take her out," he said contemptuously, dropping her into their eager arms. "You know where—same place I'm taking this here squint-eyed bastard."

Volpes palmed his revolver again and, with the third man, marched Ki outside, a few steps behind the two who were carrying Daphne. Down along the side of the cabin they went, and openly across the clearing. Daphne had begun to regain her senses by now, groggily staggering between the two men, whimpering as they fondled her breasts and fingered her loins, still damp from Ki's secretions.

The clearing lay bleak under an overcast sky, cooled by a leaden drizzle and shadowed by the advance of evening. Only ten or so rustlers were out of their shacks, most of them milling about the fire to warm themselves. Whey they glimpsed Daphne and Ki being paraded naked past them, their first reaction was one of astonishment. But when they saw how the two nude prisoners were being mauled and manhandled, they quickly began jeering and hooting obscenities.

"Get an eyeful now, fellas," Volpes yelled back, "'cause this'll be the last you'll be seeing of 'em!" Then, jabbing Ki in the spine with the muzzle of his revolver, he said in a lower but nastier voice, "Ryker'll fart a blue streak when he finds out. But I'll just tell him you were too tricky to let run around loose."

They entered the scrub at the other side of the clearing, where thorny vines and briars scraped Ki's bare legs as he was prodded up a rocky defile. He walked without giving resistance, without showing any defiance, while his mind worked swiftly to figure out when and where to make his stand. But mainly he walked feeling sadness for Daphne and bitterness toward himself. The gleam in Volpes's eyes was of pure malicious hatred—the implacably murderous kind that Daphne had warned him Volpes would feel—and that now was directed against them both. Yet Ki understood this kind of hatred, and in a sense he could not blame Volpes for it. In fact, he held a certain rueful respect for it.

Fifty yards from the clearing, Volpes called a halt in a wide spot of the defile. The ground was relatively soft here, a bit sandy and fit only for grass and stubby weeds—and for three oblong mounds of earth, just beginning to sprout fresh growth.

A rusty shovel was stuck like a grave marker at the end of one of the mounds. Volpes crossed over, still covering Ki with his revolver, and with his free hand he wriggled the shovel loose.

"Here," he ordered, handing Ki the shovel. "Now dig."

★

Chapter 15

Ki took the shovel and rubbed his hands along its rough wooden handle. He considered it in terms of a weapon; and then he wondered about the three victims already buried here, who they'd been and if they'd thought the same thing about the shovel while digging their own graves.

"Go on, start digging," Volpes snapped. "Right where you're standing will do fine, I reckon."

Ki glanced fleetingly at Daphne, who still needed to be held upright, her face a mask of mute terror. Then he began to dig. Under the thin top layer of soil, the shovel struck clay pan, and his digging became more difficult. The evening lengthened; Ki's naked chest and back soon became beaded with sweat, which riveted down his flesh and mixed with the drizzly rain. By the end of an hour, he had gouged a three-by-six pit to the depth of a foot.

"Keep digging," Volpes growled. "But I'll let you off

easy. You don't have to dig two holes, just make yours double-wide."

The two men flanking Daphne chuckled snidely; they were smugly relaxed after an hour of waiting, and Daphne was giving them no trouble. She was slumped in despair between them, speechless and glassy-eyed with her mounting horror. The third man was leaning against a boulder directly across the pit from Ki, holding his pistol lazily in his lap and appearing to be bored stiff. Volpes was a couple of yards to the near side of the man, facing Ki as alertly as ever, keeping his revolver leveled and taking no chances that his prisoner might attempt a break.

Ki continued digging. When the dual grave was a foot deeper and wider, he was positive he and Daphne would be shot firing-squad style and dumped into it, to be covered over and never found again. Whatever he was going to do, he'd have to do in the next few seconds.

"Enough digging," Volpes said suddenly, as if reading Ki's thoughts. "Okay, boys, bring the bitch over next to him."

The two hauled Daphne closer, while the other man, now holding his pistol firmly, rose and moved beside Volpes. Daphne was now mewing and writhing feebly, and when Ki said to her sharply, *"Tao Nien Hou,"* he couldn't be sure whether she was nodding with understanding, or merely shuddering with mind-numbing dread. But it was too late to repeat; it had either sunk in or not, and if not, they were both virtually dead. Volpes and the man beside him were foolishly close together, but that still left Ki's back exposed to the two men holding Daphne.

"That's it," Volpes was snarling in response to Ki's words, "Say your yaller prayers." And he thumbed back the hammer . . .

And Ki dove across the pit, gripping the shovel lengthwise by its handle. A thunderous flash exploded before him, the heavy .45 slug whispering past his ear as it sped harmlessly into the woods. Before Volpes could trigger again, before the man beside him could fire his own pistol, Ki had leaped the short space and flattened Volpes with a combination of shovel to the face and flying kick to the chest. The wooden handle smashed between Volpes's upper lip and nostrils with a driving upward thrust, shattering his nose and spearing shards of bone and cartilage into his brain. This, while Ki's driving feet were crushing his chest, snapping ribs into his lungs and rupturing his stomach and kidneys.

Volpes was dead before he hit the ground, and Ki was attacking the other man. He seemed to pivot in midair, using the shovel again to swipe the man's gun-wrist with a lightning sideways chop, and all in the same motion, as the pistol dropped and discharged, he added a thumb-jab to the man's neck. The man began wilting, his brain bursting from the eruptive pressure on his carotid artery. Lurching, spinning, dying, he fell backward into the open pit.

Again Ki swiveled, bracing himself against the expected fusillade of bullets from the men behind him. But Daphne had heard him, had understood, and with courage born of hope and desperation, had reacted the instant he'd sprung into action.

She had been forced to the edge of the grave by the man on her right, who was pulling her by the wrist, and the man on her left, who had a grip on her elbow. In response to Ki's barked command, she had applied *Tao Nien Hou*—the *T'ai-chi* maneuver that translates as "Step Back to Repulse the Monkey." She simply let her left elbow relax, dropping it into the man's grip—which, by removing all resistance, threw him immediately off balance, causing him to stumble. At the same moment, she placed all her weight in her left leg, extending her right palm in a forward thrust to the chest of the man holding her wrist. He had been pulling her, so the last thing he expected was for that hand suddenly to come toward him with lightning speed, as it now did. He also stumbled, and let go of her wrist.

Confused, the two men pounced for her again. Daphne barely had time to ward off one by striking his face with her left palm, when the other closed with a bear hug. She evaded his right arm by pushing it aside with her left forearm, and then, swiftly following through with the *Shih Tzŭ Shou* or "Cross Hands" movement, she simultaneously stabbed her right hand forward over her left forearm, her extended fingers rupturing the man's trachea just below the thyroid gland. The man clawed at his neck, strangling...

But his partner, swearing, was bearing down on Daphne with his Colt .44-40, squeezing the trigger before she could turn...

And Ki came launching across the pit again in a *tomoenage* whirl, caroming into him, sending the man sprawling on his back. Desperately the man tried straightening, aiming the pistol he still gripped tenaciously in his fist. Ki feinted with a kick, as if to knock the pistol away, and the man responded as Ki anticipated, rolling back to gain more space. Half through his roll and facedown, the man suddenly felt Ki jump on his back, and then he felt excruciating pain, and then nothing, as Ki grabbed both his ankles and pulled violently up and backward. A scream, a dull cracking noise, and the man died, his back broken and his spinal cord severed.

Daphne rushed to Ki, almost collapsing with relief into his comforting arms. "Oh, I was so terrified," she whimpered, clinging tightly to him.

"You did beautifully," Ki soothed her, cradling her head to his chest. "You're a little rusty with your timing, but you did just fine."

"I know. I should practice more. My father would be ashamed." She drew away then, her eyes bright disks of fear and excitement. "Ki, we've got to get out of here, and fast!"

Before Ki could answer, other voices starting filtering from the clearing:

"Boss?"

"Hey, you all right?"

"Boss, what's going on there?"

Then came the noise of boots approaching through the brush.

A low word came from Daphne's lips. Ki touched her to warn her that silence was necessary, holding on to her right arm as he guided her out of the defile and into the sheltering woods. But he was aware that she was right. The very compactness of the pocket would make any possible refuge out of the question for long. Daylight would, of course, make them easy game for the remaining rustlers.

"Crap, looky here!"

"They got the boss!"

"They got everyone!"

Ki dropped low to the ground, Daphne stretching close beside him. "If we can, we should circle back to the shed," he whispered in her ear, "and try for our clothes. What there is of them."

"Goddammit, they've escaped!"

"Where?"

"They can't have gone far. They gotta still be in here someplace, so let's block the hole before they can get out it."

"Yeah, four of us can do that."

"Me an' Clyde, we'll stake out that shed."

"Good idea. Some of you help me build up the fire so we can see 'em, and then let's spread out, track 'em down."

So much for getting out the simple way, Ki thought glumly, or for getting back to the shed for their clothes. "We'd better find a good place to hide," he said to Daphne.

In a crouching run, they wormed through the low scrub and trees toward the nearest slope of the pocket, ducking before they reached it and lying down prone, motionless, as four men trampled past, heading for the entrance hole.

The campfire was flaring briskly now, as kindling, brush, and tree limbs were tossed on it. Across the pocket, Ki and Daphne reached the steep, rocky wall, anxiously watching the growing flames brighten the encroaching night darkness. They moved along the slope, exploring the stone with their hands and bare feet, hoping, praying to locate enough rubble to hide in. The light was growing in the pocket, casting reflections almost to the walls. In a few more minutes it would be light everywhere. They must be undercover by then.

Cautiously they continued groping along. The pile played out, and for the space of a hundred feet, they encountered no more loose rock at all. Growing desperate, Ki went straight down the side wall and around to the one supporting the land-bridge that concealed the pocket. Daphne kept close beside him, touching him occasionally as if for support. Nothing. Nothing at all. Still they moved on, hurrying more, running out of time.

They almost bumped into a rough jumble of boulders that seemed to jut out of nowhere. Signaling Daphne to wait, Ki moved around it, searching its contours with his fingers. He came to a narrow crevice that angled in to the face of the wall like a wedge.

"I think we might have found a hiding place," he whispered to Daphne when he returned. "Maybe it won't last long, but it's something."

He also thought they must be so close to the land-bridge that any guard posted up on its rim would surely notice them when the fire rose full enough. That there would be a guard, or guards, was something Ki could almost certainly count on; Volpes couldn't have lasted as long as he had, if he hadn't taken elementary precautions like that. Yet by shifting some of the stones, Ki was able to fashion a place for them to lie flat. No part of the pile of stone was high, but it would conceal them from a distance.

The rustlers were already divided up into teams, and were impatiently scouring the pocket from one end to the other. One group, reaching the exit that led through the land-bridge, called out, "Hey, Johnson! McCully! What're you doin'—sleepin'?"

"Hell, no!" a loud bellow replied. "We're right here on this side of the hole, and Winnie and Sam are on t'other. A field mouse ain't gonna get by us. What's up? You lost 'em?"

"Naw, we just ain't found 'em yet, is all."

"We'll ride this pocket till we root 'em out," another of

the group shouted, as the men turned and moved on through the brush.

The roaring blaze from the campfire was strong enough now to illuminate the entire area, even high up the walls of the pocket. Hidden in the rocks, Ki kept surveying the slope they were against, curious about a line of blackness along it. A slight crown cast shadows far above it, but something lower down, not ten feet over their heads, also drew his close scrutiny.

After a long study, Ki decided that what he was seeing was a fault line running up the wall, a thin slice of softer stone that had eroded, crumbling, forming the rubble they were lying in now, and leaving a depression in the otherwise sheer surface of the wall.

Ki wondered if it could be climbed. Probably not, but on the other hand, they couldn't stay where they were forever. A losing proposition, no matter how he chose. He chose to try.

Touching Daphne on the shoulder, Ki slipped from his bentover crouch and began inching laborously ahead of her into the fault. She promptly, unquestioningly, followed his lead. Slowly they worked their way up the fault which was like a stovepipe cut lengthwise down the middle, bracing themselves against the thin sides of the depression with elbows and knees, exerting all their strength to retain a hold in what time-scalloped chinks they could find. They climbed and climbed, and then climbed some more, clawing with broken fingernails and tensed feet, realizing that if they should slip now, their height would guarantee a grisly death.

A second bunch of riders trotted up, and Ki and Daphne froze while the men exchanged a few words with the four guarding the hole. Then one of them stretched in his saddle to yell out, "Tait!"

When nobody responded, he shouted again, "Tait, damn your mangy hide, where the fuck are you up there? Answer me!"

Nobody did, and now another of the men said, "Ah, forget it, George. Tait's likely over watching the other side of the bridge, where Volpes told him to set tight this morning."

"Yeah, maybe, but I don't like—"

"Hell, Tait's a good egg. He'll nab 'em if'n they get up there. Which they can't, 'lessen they suddenly grow wings."

"Almost seems like they did."

"Can't find no sign of 'em in here, 'pears like."

"They've gotta be here!" George raged, wrenching his horse about. "They're lying out there laughing at us, I knows it!"

Ki and Daphne held their breaths; the men were so near the boulders below that it seemed impossible for them not to have noticed the two naked bodies clinging up in the fault. But the men all turned with the one named George, and rode back toward the clearing, where the others were gathering now, equally discouraged.

Ki surveyed the ridge above, and the surrounding cliffs, then glanced at the sky, pleased to see that the rainy overcast was blanketing the stars and moon. He craned to whisper down at Daphne, "There's a guard up there, but evidently he's posted way over by the trail leading in. There's a chance we can avoid him."

"There's a better chance I'm going to fall if you don't get moving again," she quavered.

Ki started the perilous climb again, Daphne moving right behind him with a sigh. They struggled higher as fast as they could, but the steepness and shallowness of the fault made their progress agonizingly slow.

Eventually they reached the overhang of the ridge. Ki caught the rim of the fault and flung himself over. Immediately he turned and helped Daphne over the edge. She fell forward, scrambling to her knees and then pitching forward a second time.

"Hurt?" Ki asked hoarsely.

"Out of breath. Let's get out of here."

They got three feet from the rim, when a shape loomed out of the trees directly ahead. It was a hard black outline against the softer black of the forest, and the most Ki could tell about it was that it was fat, it carried a rifle, and it was lurching toward them, babbling, "It's a trap! They think I'm helping, but—"

The shape stopped short, blurting, "You!" as Ki rushed toward it. "You again! You and that damned female!" the shape was ranting, leveling the rifle. "Least I'll pay one of you back!"

Ki didn't understand what the shape was saying, and he didn't care. He was simply assuming the shape was the guard named Tait, and that Tait would be able to shoot him before he could get the rifle.

"Here's lead in your guts!" the shape yelled.

And from behind Ki, Daphne threw a large rock, which beaned the shape smack in the middle of the forehead. The shape grunted in shock and pain, collapsing backwards into the brush with a resounding crash, his nerveless trigger finger twitching just enough to discharge the rifle into the air.

And all hell broke loose.

Volleys of rifle fire poured down into the pocket from the surrounding cliffs, lances of flame sizzling from the blackness and raking the clearing. The rustlers below reacted with desperate swiftness. No more than three had fallen from where they'd been gathering around the huge campfire, before the others spurred their horses for the brush or dove for the cover of the shacks and rocks. And even while seeking shelter, the rustlers were managing to return the fire, scattering a few shots at first, then retaliating fully.

Shocked and baffled, Ki and Daphne leaped for the brush into which their mysterious assailant had fallen.

"Where did all that shooting come from?" Daphne asked, bewildered.

"I have no idea," Ki said, "but somehow you managed to knock out Deputy Oakes."

"A *lawman?* Oh, no!"

"Oh, yes. But beggars can't be choosers." Grabbing Oakes by one leg, Ki pulled him closer and then began to hurredly yank off his boots. "Quick, help me with his clothes," Ki told Daphne, unbuckling the gunbelt. "You get his shirt, I'll take his pants."

The deputy was stripped to his flannel underwear, while the gun battle raged around them. The hidden riflemen on the perimeter of the pocket were pumping bullet after bullet at the slightest glimpse of exposed flesh. And the rustlers were replying with a barrage of their own. From the shacks, rocks, and scrub, they were sending a shower of lead up into the cliffs. Some tried to bolt out through the entrance hole, but were blocked by bullets and forced back into the pocket.

There were other men on the floor of the pocket who were still out in the open. They were thrashing with wounds or dying in the muddy dirt. But for the most part, the rustlers were retaliating with withering brutality. Lead spanged and howled off the boulders and trees ringing the cliffs.

Impossible or not, Ki and Daphne had to brave it. Cursing, Ki began loping deeper into the brush, clasping Oakes's tentlike pants around his waist. Daphne, pausing on impulse to scoop up the deputy's rifle, then sprinted after him, the shirt flapping around her like some wide dress with too high a hemline.

There was no time for stealth. They ran toward the opposite side of the cliffs, veering diagonally to the left when they spotted a bouldered slope dipping down into the canyon, far enough away from the waterfall to miss most of the action centered there.

But some of the gunmen below turned from firing at the rustlers who were trying to get out the entry hole, and began blasting away at Ki and Daphne. Exposed on the steeply slanting hill and appearing to be running away—which they were—they were prime targets for the unknown attackers. Friend or foe, Ki had no way of knowing, and he wasn't about to try stopping to ask. Lead sang and ricocheted around the pair as they charged zigzagging down the slope. A bullet showered pieces of stone in his face, and he ducked reflexively, feeling a shard stab into his neck. He ignored it, seeing ahead where some horses stood tethered.

A handful of the gunmen broke from around the waterfall and came rushing forward with guns blazing to cut Ki and Daphne off. Clasping her hand, Ki fairly whipped Daphne off her feet as they raced for the horses, bullets buzzing around them. They only had time to grab one, Ki judged—the closest one, a moro with tan leggings.

Ki hoisted Daphne into the saddle, hurled himself at the reins, then flung himself up in front of her. Fighting the spooked, rearing horse, he shouted, "Hang on!" and jabbed both heels into the moro's ribs.

The moro bolted straight down the creek as a barrage of shots pursued them. Just to keep the pursuing mob respectful, Daphne twisted around and, with one hand clutching the waist of the wide-bottomed pants Ki was wearing, fired the rifle. She fired only once, there being no way she could lever a new round and still keep her balance.

"Throw that thing away and keep down," Ki cautioned, feeling bullets clip past him. "All you're doing is making them madder."

Riding furiously, they galloped away from the hail of lead. Scattered shots chased them as they reached the mouth of the canyon and pounded into the hills beyond. The shots did not cease until they were long out of sight and range.

After another quarter-mile, Ki slowed the horse, which was lathered and panting under its double load. They rode on blindly, through canyons and across broken uplands, and the longer they went, the more like a labyrinth it became. They would emerge from one brush-clogged valley only to crown a barren crag that would lead into yet another canyon, with yet another bench stretching beyond that. Without the moon or stars, it was impossible to gauge their direction accurately. But by keeping the pocket and the canyon with the waterfall in a general line behind them, Ki sensed that they were heading generally eastward, and would eventually come out close to Eucher Butte.

He let the moro seek its own pace, feeling less concerned now about pursuit. Daphne squeezed tightly against him as she rode more or less on the rim of the cantle, her arms hugging Ki around his waist, her face pressed against his bare back.

"Who were those gunmen?" she asked after a while.

"I've been thinking about that. Ranchers, probably. Fed-up ranchers and their crews, who finally learned where the rustlers were camped, and decided to do something on their own about it."

"They sure are. They're finishing it for you."

"Finishing?"

"You told me in the shed you were staying because you weren't finished. Well, you got to finish Volpes—and the ranchers, or whoever they are, are finishing his gang—so what else is there?"

"Volpes's boss, Ryker. I was hoping he'd show up personally, and maybe he would have later, except Volpes wasn't going to give us a later. And I was hoping to find out where the stolen cows are."

"Oh, I know where. In a bunch of box canyons way up in the hills of the Block-Two-Dot range. You should've asked me. I overheard Volpes and Ryker talking about brand-blotching all the cattle they were keeping there, so when Ryker bought out the other ranches, he could restock them with the ranchers' own herds."

"No wonder none of the stolen cows ever showed up."

"But Ki, about the ranchers—why're we running from them?"

"I only *think* they're ranchers, Daphne. They're certainly not the army, and for lawmen they're lousy shots, lucky for us. But, ranchers or not, they didn't know who we are, and didn't act inclined to find out while we were still breathing. And then there was that strange stuff Deputy Oakes was babbling..." Ki paused, then added, "Besides, did you want all those men to catch you naked?"

"No."

"The newspapers would have gobbled it up. 'Nude Queen of the Outlaws Captured in Shootout.' You have have had a hell of a time getting a fresh start, with that bandied about." Hastily, Ki amended, "Don't get me wrong,

Daphne, I'm laying no claim to change you. Do exactly what suits you best. I'm only saying... well, maybe this way you've got a choice you didn't have before."

There was a giggle. "Your neck's turning red."

"No, it's not. Not me. Actually, the more I think about it, the more I'm changing my mind. I'm taking you in for charges."

Daphne gasped. "Me? You're having me arrested?"

"You bet. Serious offense too. They'll probably hang you for it. Stoning a law officer while he was performing his duties."

"I see. Is that worse than horse-thieving?"

"Hm, you've got a point. On third thought, you're too pretty and I'm too young to be strung up. Maybe by the time we've found our way to Eucher Butte, we'll have figured out an arrangement."

Daphne kissed him lightly on the spine, a purr to her voice. "I'm all for giving it a try." Her fingers coiled down from his waist and slithered inside the baggy top of Ki's borrowed pants, burrowing deep to touch his manhood. Gently she began stroking the fleshy shaft.

Ki felt himself responding, growing painfully rigid. And he realized that, whore or not, Daphne was not merely acting passionate now, she was genuinely aroused and eager. She simply loved making love! Obligingly, he leaned back slightly to allow her more room, her talented fondling driving him wild. She unbuttoned his fly.

Now Ki was open and exposed to Daphne's squeezing massage. Rarely had he felt so hard, so thick and throbbing, and he reined in sharply by a grassy knoll. "Daphne, at least let go of me long enough so we can get down, will you?"

Daphne had other notions. "Why dismount to mount?" she murmured, and with agile grace she hooked her left leg across his hips, and began sliding around from the cantle. Poised almost facing Ki by the front of the seat, she gently drew out his aching erection and cupped his sensitive scrotum with her other hand. "Now scrunch back. I've got the saddlehorn in places I'd rather not."

Ki moved up onto the cantle, while Daphne balanced on her knees to rise over his thighs. Deputy Oakes's pants were so large on Ki that, despite being stretched by Ki straddling the horse, the open flaps of the front lay wide and unhindering. Rolling the tail of her shirt out of the way, Daphne looked down between their bellies at their coupling. Then, guiding him in with one hand, she slipped down the full length of her haunches to squat blissfully impaled upon his shaft. "Ahhh...!" she cooed, smiling rapturously.

The horse, misunderstanding the motions of her thighs and legs, began slowly trotting forward again. Head arched and mouth wide to emit sighs of raw pleasure, Daphne swiftly matched her pumping rhythm with the easy tempo of the horse's gait. She strained against Ki, her arms clutching him tightly around his back, while inside, Ki could feel his urgency burgeoning with every surge of her satiny sheath. He was hardly aware of anything but the incredible sensations of the thrusting, compounding movements as he held her upright, tonguing her breasts, hearing her whimpers.

And as the horse jogged through the meandering canyon, and they jogged along with it, Ki realized dimly, peripherally, that the slopes were broadening and the land ahead was widening. Glancing fleetingly over Daphne's heaving shoulders, he vaguely saw, beyond an intervening ridge, plumes of smoke lifting against the gray drizzly sky. Eucher Butte, it had to be.

"We're almost out," he whispered, tonguing her ear.

"You're in," she whimpered. "I can feel you, deep."

"Out of the hills. And what a way to go."

"Yes..." Again she whimpered.

"We're going out with a whimper *and* a bang."

★

Chapter 16

"How d'you expect me to go arrestin' properly," Deputy Oakes was complaining, "when I'm wearin' only my long-johns?"

"You'd better get to doing your duty right snappy," Daryl Melville retorted, "before you lose them too. Making us believe you were going to help, so we'd uncuff you! And give you a rifle! Then hightailing it away, sneaking around on your fat carcass!"

"Well, I was gonna fight!" Oakes rubbed the middle of his forehead, where clotted blood gave him the appearance of having a red third eye. "I did, too. Struggled somethin' fierce when that howling mob attacted me, but I was over-powered and knocked out."

"Howling mob!" Toby Melville scoffed. "You tripped."

"No such! And I didn't snitch m'own horse, neither."

They were standing in the front room of the outlaws' log

cabin, feeling agitated and pumped up in the aftermath of their successful battle. A few men were with them, guarding a half-dozen wounded rustlers, who were slouched grimacing with pain and brooding over the fate they knew awaited them. The combined ranches' crews were still combing the pocket, remorselessly hunting the stubborn holdouts of Volpes's now shattered gang.

Jessica entered from the clearing, her arms filled with Ki's clothing. She placed the bundle on the table, alongside his daggers, his jammed *shuriken* devices, and his other weaponry, which she'd found in a rear room of the cabin. Then, stalking over to the nearest rustler, she demanded with cold fury, "What have you done with him?"

The rustler looked up with filmy eyes. "Who? The gent Volpes brung here?" Pink spittle drooled from his mouth. "Nothin'. He killed Volpes and vamoosed, just afore you laid into us."

Jessica sighed, relieved. "He's alive."

The man coughed. "With a gal."

"A girl?" Daryl blurted. "A lady was here too?"

"It figures," Jessica said, recalling the nightgown she'd found in the shed with Ki's clothing. "If there's a woman within a fifty miles, Ki will somehow get to her."

"Nekkid," the man said, coughing again.

Jessica nodded. "That figures too. He's safe, anyway."

"Safe? Jessie, your friend could be out there anywhere in those wild hills, lost, wandering, catching pneumonia!"

"Leave it lie, Daryl. If Ki's out there naked with a woman," Jessica said wearily, "he'll do fine. No, I'm not so worried about Ki right now. What I'm worried about is that we haven't much time left and we've got to act fast."

"Doing what?" Toby asked, his old face wrinkling with perplexity. "We done what we come for. We stomped these snakes good."

"We've only cut off one end of the snake," Jessica explained. "The rest of its body and head are still very much alive at the Block-Two-Dot. And it'll all wriggle away if we don't stop it."

Daryl gasped. "You mean another raid?"

"Yes, now, as quickly as we can, before Ryker gets wind of what's happened here. If we don't, if he and his men escape, then mark my words, that snake will soon grow another full-sized body."

Daryl grinned and touched his revolver. "You're right, Jessie, and I'm all for it. Let me round up the boys and we'll ride. But what about things here? There's still some mopping up."

"You hit leather, son," Toby said. "I reckon me an' a few Flying W hands can manage what's left."

"Good," Jessica said. "Let's waste no more time. Come on, Daryl. And you too, Oakes, you look in need of an education."

They trooped out the door, the deputy following glumly.

It didn't take long for the crews to be mustered, and voicing their support, they lined out toward the hole out of the pocket. Four of them remained behind to help Toby Melville track down and ride herd on the few surviving rustlers, one of them lending his Flying W mount to a reluctant and melancholy Deputy Oakes.

Once past the waterfall, the riders set a fast pace with Daryl leading the way, Jessica beside him. The miles flowed steadily by, and their unflagging persistence paid off; shortly before midnight, they reached the rugged barrier between the foothills and the flat range bordering the Block-Two-Dot ranch. Daryl now led them in a wide arc away from the direct trail, easing into the sloping, round-shouldered valley grassland in front of the ranch in such a manner as to avoid any Block-Two-Dot crewmen who might be out.

At last Daryl held up his hand as a signal to draw up. The men clustered around him as he explained, "We can't surround the ranch like we did the pocket, but we don't have to, either. The way those high cliffs enclose it on three sides, all we've got to do is spread out and strike all at once along the open front."

"We'll handle it like before," Jessica added. "Nobody make any move until you hear us fire one shot."

"Say," a crewman asked, "who gave the signal last time?"

Silence. Deputy Oakes sat like a stone in the saddle.

"Doesn't matter," Daryl said. "Just remember, when it comes, hit hard with all you've got. They'll be slinging a heap of lead, I imagine, but we've got surprise on our side. Understand?"

A low muttering of agreement answered him.

Jessica and Daryl veered toward the right, making sure the deputy was trailing close by. The crews spread out in an angular line, then advanced cautiously toward the ranch.

The Block-Two-Dot was not as quiet or dark as it had been the night Jessica had first seen it. Light glimmered from the bunkhouse and barn, and the main house windows were ablaze with lamps. A big freight wagon was in the yard, and men were carrying wooden crates out of the house and stacking them in the wagon bed. Another group was loafing next to the wagon, smoking cigarettes and watching the loading, while still other men were saddling horses in the corral.

Puzzled, Daryl turned to Jessica. "What're they doing?"

"Getting ready to pull out," Jessica said quietly. "I don't know how Ryker learned about our raid on the pocket—maybe one of the rustlers slipped through our trap, or one of his crewmen was riding there and saw what was happening—but that's got to be it. He's pulling up stakes, and we got here in the nick of time."

"Then let's hit 'em," Daryl said impatiently. He spurred his buckskin forward, triggering his revolver to signal the others.

Instantly the crewmen surged into action along their line facing the ranch. The long crescent of thundering guns swept in like an avenging tidal wave toward the Block-Two-Dot yard.

Ryker's renegade ranch hands, as vicious and callous an outlaw breed as the rustlers, were caught unawares. With yells of shock and pain, they turned to defend their exposed flanks, some digging in to fire a deadly answer to the riders' challenge, while others dove behind the wagon or into the buildings, blasting back against the onslaught of grimly determined men.

The line charged into the yard, turning the ranch into an inferno of pounding hoofs, rearing horses, roaring guns. Twice Ryker's crew recoiled in wild pandemonium. Twice it managed to rally in its frantic effort to bust out of this ring of death. The attack became a close-quarter melee of pistols and knives and hand-to-hand struggles with those caught out in the yard and grounds, while, with neither conscience nor mercy, volley after volley riddled those trapped inside the bunkhouse and other outbuildings.

The Block-Two-Dot crew could only take so much of it. Suddenly they broke, leaping out of doors and windows in panicked retreat, fleeing headlong in every direction, scattering on foot toward the haven of dark hills. Only from one barn and the cookshack now came a few bullets, from remaining knots of desperate men.

Jessica focused her attention on the big ranch house. It had been strangely quiet all during the fight, no mad scrambling from within, no furious shooting from its windows. She wondered why. Maybe Ryker was cowering down in that torture chamber of his. And then she wondered how much of a defense he'd put up before he surrendered. Or died. She started moving toward the house, her revolver steady as she stepped out from the cover of the freight wagon. Then from the corner of her eye, she glimpsed a heavyset rider spurring out of the shadows of the barn, galloping off in the direction of the pass.

"Ryker's making a break for it!" she shouted to Daryl. "He's running out on his own men! Well, not if I can help it!"

She raced back around the freight wagon, where she'd dismounted from her horse. Perversely, the bay shied mincingly as she vaulted into the saddle, helping Ryker by causing Jessica to waste precious moments. Regaining control, she wrenched the horse about and set it into a fast pursuit, firing a slavo from her revolver at the retreating figure. But her aim was no better than anyone else's can be when shooting from the back of a frothingly galloping horse, and Ryker was hunched so low across his horse's neck that he was almost invisible.

Ryker swiveled around and fired back. His shots, too, flew wild. Jessica surged after him along the road to the pass, ignoring the bullets zinging past her. Ryker dove into the pass while he lashed his horse faster up the trail, and plunging in only moments behind, Jessica realized she was losing ground to him. His mount was fresh, rested, doubtless of thoroughbred quality, while hers was livery stable rental, of stout heart, but winded from long riding.

Ryker came in view momentarily as he crossed an open patch of the pass trail, and Jessica snapped a quick shot at him. The bullet struck rock near Ryker's head, making him hunch yet lower as he continued urging his horse onward.

Jessica still pursued him, even though her horse was panting with raspy, harsh breaths. She could feel the bay slowing under her, still game, but simply too fatigued to keep up the grueling pace. Yet she refused to give in, infuriated, recalling her own words about the head of a snake growing a new body. If Ryker escaped...

Abruptly, Ryker showed himself again, goading his horse frenziedly out of the pass, into the first draw of the foothills. Jessica raised her revolver to fire, but the hammer struck an empty chamber. She was out of ammunition.

The bay stumbled, recovered, lurched in an ungainly lope. Jessica reined in, and patted her horse's heaving flank. There was no sense in killing the animal; Ryker had already vanished around the left-hand side of a long row of boulders.

"He got away," she said sourly to herself, quivering with frustration and wrath. "The bastard got away."

★

Chapter 17

Jessica walked slowly up the hotel stairs and turned down the corridor toward her room, feeling tired, haggard, and depressed.

Passing the door to Ki's room, she caught the faint sound of a woman's giggle, which only added to her pique. She backed a step to the door and, juggling the cumbersome load she was carrying in her hands, rapped smartly on the door. The giggling stopped. A moment later, Ki opened the door and grinned out at her, naked except for the towel clasped around his waist.

"Here," Jessica said, thrusting the bundle of his clothes and weapons at him, "I believe you left these behind in your haste."

"Thanks, Jessie, so I did. Wait a minute." He disappeared with the bundle, then returned, still clad in the towel, and eased out into the hallway, sliding the door shut behind him. "Shh," he said, handing Jessica a telegram, "A girl's resting inside."

"I just bet she is," Jessica replied as she opened the telegram and read:

PRELIMINARY INVESTIGATION OF H AND K SHOW MOST RECENT EMPLOYMENT BY SENATOR TRUMBULL AS CHAUFFEUR AND BODYGUARD RESPECTIVELY STOP BOTH WITH PRIOR PETTY RECORDS BUT SUSPICION OF INVOLVEMENT IN RECENT BANK ROBBERY IS REASON GIVEN FOR DISMISSAL FROM SERVICE STOP MORE LATER STOP

"The night clerk gave it to me," Ki was saying as she read. "The telegraph operator dropped it off when you didn't come to claim it yesterday."

"A lot of good it does now," Jessica said morosely, balling the flimsy yellow paper and tossing it aside. "We wiped out the rustlers and the Block-Two-Dot crew, but Ryker himself got away. I had him, Ki, I had him so close that I could've..." She sighed. "Well, I know he came in this direction, and I've been trailing him as best I could on that poor worn-out horse of mine, but he's long gone now."

"No, he's not," Ki said, shaking his head. "As I was coming into town, I saw Ryker heading into the Thundermug Saloon. I imagine he's still there."

"But that doesn't make sense. Why would he go there?"

"Greed. Panic. Halford and Kendrick may be rivals of Ryker, and they may hate each other like poison, but they're tied together by that." Ki indicated the telegram. "By Senator Trumbull."

"Trumbull...Dilworth Trumbull..." Jessica frowned in concentration, trying to remember what she knew of the senator, but he remained an enigmatic shadow in the back of her mind.

"Trumbull's their common connection, Jessie," Ki continued. "How, I don't know, but I suspect that since they're

171

linked to the same scheme, Halford and Kendrick can't let Ryker fail, because that'd ruin it for them too. That's why Ryker must've gone there, to persuade them to lay their differences aside, at least long enough to save his skin and rescue the setup. And to remove us for good."

"The snake's already growing a new body," Jessica muttered to herself, and then to Ki she said, "I suddenly feel in the mood for a nightcap. At the Thundermug, to be precise."

"Hold still, I notice a thirst coming on myself." Ki went back into his room, and when he came out, he was fully dressed again.

"I trust the lady's not overly distressed about this," Jessica remarked, as they started back along the corridor to the stairs.

"Daphne accepted it in the line of duty, as she does most things," Ki replied. "No, I simply explained I had an urgent need to make a late-night visit. I didn't add that it's in repayment for the man Kendrick sent to visit you in your room."

"You knew?"

"You're quiet, Jessie, but not silent. After the man left, I followed him almost to the saloon. We had a little discussion." Ki smiled as if fond of the memory, but by the time they'd reached the lobby door, he was grim again. "I also didn't add that I wish to repay our second visitor, the one with the dynamite calling card."

"Oh, that wasn't Kendrick's doing," Jessica said as they stepped out into the street. "Daryl told me Kendrick and Halford have an option on the hotel. They would scarcely blow up their own building just to get us. And that's what those sticks would've done, if they'd exploded in my room. Thank Ryker for that trick."

"I hope to."

They moved along the boardwalk, walking slowly, noting that despite the late hour, the Thundermug was still open. It didn't appear to be doing much business; no loud voices or harsh laughter filtered out its batwings, and there were very few people around in the street.

When they were still about fifty feet from the saloon, Daryl rushed up out of the shadows and stopped them. "There you are," he said to Jessica. "That's twice now you've gone off on me."

"I did not. I said I was going after Ryker, and I am."

"Well, how could I know? When you didn't come back..." Daryl made a hapless little gesture, then grinned sheepishly. "You're all right, and that's what counts. Now, where's Ryker?"

"In the Thundermug," Ki answered. "Putting his head together with Halford and Kendrick. We thought we'd stick ours in, too."

Daryl's grin broadened.

Jessica, sensing what Daryl had in mind, shook her head firmly. "No, Daryl, I can't let you. Ryker's our game, always has been."

"Yeah, but whose ranch is in hock to what crooked gambler?" Daryl spoke with hard, vengeful relish in his voice. "If there're going to be heads knocked, Kendrick's all mine to butt. Period."

"You're getting in *over* your head, Daryl. Those are killers in there, desperate killers. This isn't going to be any picnic."

"After you, Jessie," Daryl said, opening a batwing.

"Picnic," Jessica repeated, standing there in the saloon entrance as if momentarily dazed. "Picnic..." And it was in that moment that the smoldering spark in the back of her mind burst into flame—the flame of rememberance. "That's it! I've got it!"

"Got what? Ki asked.

"Picnic in the park," Jessica replied, and walked in, now so wrapped up in the solution to the puzzling scheme that she wanted nothing more than to get it over with, fast.

The crowd was thin, and somber at the tail-end of their drinking night. The same two white-aproned bartenders were at their stations, wiping down the counter and cleaning up the backbar. Halford was still under the painting of the nude, smoking another torpedo cigar, looking as if he were rooted to the spot. Seeing Jessica, Ki, and Daryl enter, his face turned pale and he sent a worried sidelong glance at his partner, Kendrick.

Kendrick was seated at a different gaming table, this one a bit closer to the front and to the bar. He was alone, and was idly riffling a deck of cards, a whiskey bottle and a glass next to his elbow. When he caught Halford's quick glance, he looked up and gave a slight wintry smile, placing the deck aside and moving a bottle and glass over to it.

"Ryker's not in here," Daryl said to Jessica, as they walked between the tables toward the gambler. "He must be in the back."

Jessica, glancing past Kendrick, saw what Daryl meant. There was a door set in the rear wall, which would undoubtedly open into the saloon's office and private quarters. "It'll be locked," she responded in a low voice. "We'll probably have to break it in."

"Once we get past these two," Daryl added.

Ki was not walking with them. He was edging parallel to them along the far side of the large room, keeping a very close eye on Halford. He skirted around a billiard table nobody was using—then hesitated and went back to it. A pair of cue sticks were resting on the baize, and billiard balls were scattered around the surface of the table. He picked up two of the balls, palming them as he swiftly moved on.

Jessica and Daryl stopped in front of Kendrick's table; Ki halting quite a few feet in back of them, still watching Halford.

"Evenin'," Kendrick said. "Care for a hand or two?"

"I care for Ryker," Jessica snapped. "Get him."

"The good Captain Ryker hasn't blessed our establishment in ages," Kendrick said blandly. "You must be mistaken, Miss Starbuck."

"He's here. You've got him hidden in back, so you three can try figuring out ways to salvage your plans for that parkland."

Kendrick jerked erect, staring at Jessica, while behind the bar, Halford gripped the counter, the cigar tipping from his mouth. And Daryl gasped at Jessica, completely baffled.

"Parkland? Jessica, there's no park hereabouts."

"Not yet," she replied in a short, clipped tone. "But think, Daryl, that huge block on Ryker's map could only represent an area the size of an Indian reservation—or a national park. Like Yellowstone. Bigger than Yellowstone! Ryker buys the land cheap, supposedly in the name of Acme Packers; then Acme merges with American Federated Development, while Senator Trumbull rams his bill through Congress establishing the area as a national park site. Then the government is forced to buy the land from American Federated at inflated prices."

"Gawd! A nation-sized swindle!"

"An *international* swindle, Daryl. There's only one gang, one international ring of criminals wealthy enough and unscrupulous enough to be able to rig such a conspiracy. I've known for some time that Ryker works for it; and now I know that through his complicity, Senator Trumbull is another of its corrupt tools. And I remembered as I was coming in here just exactly who Trumbull is—the chairman of the Senate Committee on Military Affairs."

Kendrick, having regained his composure, sank back in his chair. "Preposterous. Insane. You don't know what you're saying."

"Oh, but I do. I know this new park would be administered by the army, as Yellowstone is. I know the army's controlled by the War Department, and that the War Department is under the thumb of Congress. Through Trumbull's position, a powerful foreign cartel will not only reap a vast fortune, but will also be able to control a sizable chunk of America and our army garrisoned on it."

"Ryker, Trumbull, foreign conspirators..." Scoffing,

Kendrick reached for his glass of whiskey. "Pipe dreams, Miss Starbuck. But even if your fantasies were true, they've nothing to do with me."

"You and Halford are up to your eyeballs in it," Jessica retorted. "You two learned of this scheme while doing Trumbull's minor dirty work in Washington. So you robbed that bank and rushed out here, spending your loot to buy and option as much of Eucher Butte as you could, figuring to cheat Ryker and American Federated the way they and Trumbull are figuring to cheat our government—by squeezing them for all they're worth when they try to buy you out."

"But Jessica, Kendrick hasn't taken my ranch."

"Don't yóu see, Daryl?" Jessica cried. "He would have, as soon as it came time to sell it to Ryker or American Federated. Till then he doesn't need it, he doesn't want it. He'd let you keep running it, while making sure your father stayed strapped in his debt."

"Yeah, I see now, Jessica." Daryl leaned across the table, facing Kendrick. "I see it's more'n a swindle, it's treason." His dark eyes were icy and bright, and there was no concealing the hatred he felt for the gambler seated before him.

Kendrick pursed his pouty lips and flicked his gaze for an instant past Daryl to the bar. Halford eased closer along the counter, his hands now dipping below and out of sight. A deep hush held the room, as the few drinkers present hastily pressed back out of the line of fire. The silence held, growing, tensing like a wire on the verge of snapping...

Kendrick broke first. Cursing, he plunged his hand inside his coat for his stubby-barreled belly-gun. Daryl immediately dropped into a crouch, clawing for his old revolver, while Jessica swiveled aside and made to draw her custom .38. The customers and two bartenders dove for cover. Halford stayed where he was, his hands bringing up a sawed-off Ithaca double-barreled shotgun.

Kendrick, the first to break, was the first to fire. He

176

misjudged in his haste, and the .32 slug from his Harrington & Richardson's Vest Pocket Self-Cocker plowed a furrow along the green felt of the table, a scant inch from Daryl's side. Daryl was still hauling out his Remington, ignoring the shot and heedless of another, his motions slow and methodical and virtually suicidal.

Yet the practiced speed of Kendrick's draw and fire was even too great for Jessica to match. She realized in that split second that she wouldn't be able to level and shoot before the gambler triggered a second time. And their backs were to Halford, and Halford was aiming his shotgun squarely at Jessica and Daryl, who were standing perfectly targeted for the two unchoked 12-gauge shells in its breech. Unfortunately for him, Ki was already throwing one of the billiard balls. Ki had begun his pitch at the same moment he saw Kendrick twitch his arm toward his coat. The ball smacked Halford in the mouth, sending gold-filled teeth flying with the sound of snapping tree branches.

Halford started falling, taking the shotgun with him and accidentally discharging one of its barrels. The blast flew high, shattering one of the chandeliers hanging from the ceiling near Kendrick's card table, the spray of glass and kerosene distracting Kendrick for a second. And Daryl shot him between the eyes. The gambler lurched and slumped to the table, spilling the glass and bottle and deck of cards, his snub-nosed pistol hitting the floor.

Ki killed Halford with his second toss, a whiplashing overhand that hurled the ball like an arrow. It struck Halford, who was still crumpling from the first ball, in the forehead and crushed the frontal plate of his skull. Fitting, Ki thought as he watched Halford plummet out of sight; it seemed somehow right to repeat the stoning Daphne had given Deputy Oakes.

"The door!" Daryl shouted at Jessica, lunging past Kendrick toward the rear. He never slowed, but rammed into the back door with his left shoulder, tearing the door loose

177

from its hinges and popping its lock. He surged into the room with Jessica on his heels, their revolvers braced in their fists.

Two burly men were in the room, neither of them Ryker. Daryl cracked the first man in the face with the barrel of his revolver, but couldn't reach Jessica in time to save her from being attacked.

The second man, partially concealed behind the opening door, had leaped out and snagged Jessica by her gun-arm, and was savagely attempting to wrestle her pistol away. She wrenched back, kicking and scratching, but was unable to break free or bring her Colt to bear. In their struggle, she stumbled back against a bureau, almost upsetting it. Frantically she fought for her balance, clawing the bureau with her other hand, her fingers closing around the handle of a china water jug teetering on the bureau's top. She scooped up the jug and bashed the man over the head with it.

It was enough to send the man staggering, and Daryl dropped him with a bullet through the knee, then grinned at Jessica, and sprang for the partially open window along the far wall.

"Ryker may've gotten out here," he said, raising the sash and poking his head out. But all he saw outside was Ki.

For Ki, back in the saloon, had had a different idea where Ryker might have gone. While Jessica and Daryl had run for the door, on the assumption that Ryker had locked himself in the rear quarters, Ki had the feeling that Ryker was already out and making his escape.

Sprinting in the opposite direction, out the front of the saloon, he veered around the side toward the weedy lot that abutted the rear of the building. He skirted a stack of beer kegs and jumped up onto a small loading platform, raised about four feet off the ground. Just past the platform were three horses, and Gurthied Ryker was mounting the middle one, while two other men stood cinching their saddles.

Ryker had his revolver out. "Damned Starbuck meddlers!" he snarled, and triggered his revolver three times, very fast.

178

Ki twisted in a low, rolling circle; the first of Ryker's bullets struck a beer keg, and the second splintered the platform deck between Ki's legs. The third went straight down into the earth next to Ryker's horse, because by then a thin, tapering dagger was protruding from Ryker's chest.

Ryker coughed, shaking from the impact of Ki's thrown dagger. He started mounting higher but couldn't quite make his saddle, and for a moment he clung with his hands grasping the horn, then slumped back.

The man on his left had danced away from the horses, and had dropped to his knee to sight his revolver. He was hunching like that, steadying his revolver, when a bullet from the rear window struck him in the side and toppled him over.

The third man fled out across the back lot, losing all interest in the confrontation.

Rising from the deck of the platform, Ki dropped off onto the ground and walked over to Ryker. The man remained in his strange position, a boot in one stirrup, both hands grasping the saddlehorn, the index finger of his right hand curled around the trigger of his revolver, preventing the pistol from falling. His whole body had a soft, sagging appearance to it. When Ki loosened Ryker's hands, the man crumpled to the ground, as if deflating.

Ki removed his dagger, wiped its blade on Ryker's shirt, and slipped it back into its pocket on the inside of his vest. Then, from another pocket, Ki took out one of his *shuriken;* he'd purposely brought it along for just this occasion, having taken it from his jammed device before leaving his hotel room. Bending down, he stuck one star-pointed edge into the dagger wound as a memento, as a warning sign to other members of the cartel. Straightening then, he walked to the front of the saloon.

Jessica and Daryl were waiting for him outside the batwings. "Daryl pegged one from the window," Jessica said. "I didn't realize he could shoot that well at an angle."

"I didn't either," Daryl said. "Was it Ryker?"

"No, but Ryker's dead," Ki replied. "I'm glad you got

the one you did, though, because the man was about set to peg me."

They started down the boardwalk toward the hotel, as Daryl ejected spent cartridges from his Remington. "I guess that takes care of that, then. You'll be leaving tomorrow, back to Texas?"

Ki didn't answer. Jessica also didn't respond for a long moment, but finally said, "Well, we might have to stay over for the inquest. There's sure to be one held, don't you think?"

"If not, there should be," Daryl answered, cheering.

"Plus the investigation," Ki added.

"Into the rustling and parkland swindle?"

"No, Daryl, I had more in mind into how Deputy Oakes's horse got from the canyon to the livery stable. Not to mention the disappearance of his clothes. I doubt he'll have forgotten that."

"Not much to fret over," Jessica said. "After tonight, the deputy's goose has been burnt to a frazzle." She turned to smile at Daryl. "Since we'll probably be staying in Eucher Butte a few more days, maybe we should spend it searching for your stock."

"I know where the stolen herds are. Up in some box canyons at the far end of Ryker's ranch," Ki said, then he let out a wearied sigh. "I'm not feeling up to it, I'm afraid. I need a rest."

"That is a shame," Jessica consoled. "Well, you just stay resting up in your room. But my, I do dislike riding alone."

Daryl moistened his lips. "Reckon I might be able to fill in. They are my cows, after all." He reflected a bit longer, then suggested, "How 'bout if I slept over the night at the hotel, and me and you take a ride over thataway after breakfast tomorrow?"

"Whatever you think best," Jessica said primly.

"Good," Ki remarked with a flicker of a smile as they stepped into the lobby of the hotel. "I can see everybody is going to get a hell of a rest."

Longarm fans gather round—
The biggest Longarm ever is
riding your way!

LONGARM
AND THE
LONE STAR LEGEND

The Wild West will never be the same! The first giant Longarm saga is here and you won't want to miss it. LONGARM AND THE LONE STAR LEGEND features rip-snortin' action with Marshall Long, and introduces a sensational new heroine for a new kind of Western adventure that's just rarin' to please. Jessie Starbuck's her name and satisfaction's her game...and any man who stands in her way had better watch out!

So pull on your boots and saddle up for the biggest, boldest frontier adventure this side of the Pecos. Order today!

0-515-06225-1/$2.75

Explore the exciting Old West with one of the men who made it wild!

_____ 06157-3	LONGARM AND THE RAILROADERS #24	$1.95
_____ 05974-9	LONGARM ON THE OLD MISSION TRAIL #25	$1.95
_____ 06952-3	LONGARM AND THE DRAGON HUNTERS #26	$2.25
_____ 06158-1	LONGARM AND THE RURALES #27	$1.95
_____ 06629-X	LONGARM ON THE HUMBOLDT #28	$2.25
_____ 05585-9	LONGARM ON THE BIG MUDDY #29	$1.95
_____ 06581-1	LONGARM SOUTH OF THE GILA #30	$2.25
_____ 06580-3	LONGARM IN NORTHFIELD #31	$2.25
_____ 06582-X	LONGARM AND THE GOLDEN LADY #32	$2.25
_____ 06583-8	LONGARM AND THE LAREDO LOOP #33	$2.25
_____ 06584-6	LONGARM AND THE BOOT HILLERS #34	$2.25
_____ 06630-3	LONGARM AND THE BLUE NORTHER #35	$2.25
_____ 06953-1	LONGARM ON THE SANTA FE #36	$1.95
_____ 06954-X	LONGARM AND THE STALKING CORPSE #37	$2.25
_____ 06955-8	LONGARM AND THE COMANCHEROS #38	$2.25
_____ 05594-8	LONGARM AND THE DEVIL'S RAILROAD #39	$1.95
_____ 05596-4	LONGARM IN SILVER CITY #40	$1.95
_____ 05597-2	LONGARM ON THE BARBARY COAST #41	$1.95
_____ 05598-0	LONGARM AND THE MOONSHINERS #42	$1.95
_____ 05599-9	LONGARM IN YUMA #43	$2.25
_____ 05600-6	LONGARM IN BOULDER CANYON #44	$2.25
_____ 05601-4	LONGARM IN DEADWOOD #45	$2.25
_____ 05602-2	LONGARM AND THE GREAT TRAIN ROBBERY #46	$2.25
_____ 05603-0	LONGARM IN THE BADLANDS #47	$2.25

Available at your local bookstore or return this form to:

J **JOVE/BOOK MAILING SERVICE**
P.O. Box 690, Rockville Center, N.Y. 11570

Please enclose 75¢ for postage and handling for one book, 25¢ each
add'l. book ($1.50 max.). No cash, CODs or stamps. Total amount
enclosed: $ _____ in check or money order.

NAME _____

ADDRESS _____

CITY _____ STATE/ZIP _____

Allow six weeks for delivery. SK-6